Love,

Home,

and

By Alexei McConville

ISBN: 978-1-66784-753-5
e-ISBN: 978-1-66784-754-2

Edited by Arlene McConville
Cover Art designed by Alexei McConville
Published using the services of and Printed and Distributed by Bookbaby.com

Printed in the United States of America

https://www.patreon.com/alexeimcconville

Table of Contents

Introductions to the Uncertain City

Located somewhere in the State of Washington, found along an ocean inlet, hidden in a perpetual and impenetrable fog, is a city of sixty thousand that has two names, Darkess Noir. The names encapsulate everything that is and shall ever be 'The Unknown.' Explicitly suitable for the city that bears the strange and mysterious.

There is no denying the fact that the city goes unnoticed by the world. The impending miasma seems to hide the place away in a dimension beyond attention. Even neighboring counties do not notice what is right beside them. And, once within the limits, everything outside becomes non-existent. Though, even with this feeling of isolation, numerous people find themselves passing through, coming to visit, and moving here for no explicable reason. They have been drawn by the mysteries waiting to be discovered.

Many stories, both humorous and horrifying, circulate through the ethos. These urban legends have become essential to the way of life for those that have made this place their home. That is because the weird and bizarre have long since taken on a life of their own. There is not always an easy explanation for things that happen around the city. Often, logic must be disregarded, or else people will begin to go mad trying to understand why.

'Why' is a dangerous thought. The question leaves much to be wondered and wanted. People are driven to pointlessly seek something that can provide an explanation to relieve feeling incomplete. Yet, answers will never truly be found here. That uncertainty is what stays with us afterward. That uncertainty is the reason many have stayed.

The feeble, unfortunate, and lethargic are the ones trapped in Darkess. They have become habitual inhabitants deeply planted in the city to the point that they can no longer escape. The world outside is too different, too ordinary. Normalcy has become abnormal. Whereas abnormality is now the expected standard. Wallowing here is what remains for these poor souls. They have been permanently twisted. Never will they be able to function anywhere else. That is not to say the city is filled with malice and dread that forces the residents to abandon all hope and be consumed by their anxiety.

On the contrary, the private and curious nature of Noir creates excitement and adventure for those that are not afraid to look into the abyss. Drifters, that tend to be seeking meaning outside the traditional expectations of life, those who have traveled the country or even the world, eventually wind up here. Intellectuals holding deep philosophical ideas, those who want to delve even deeper into the profound metaphysics, begin here. Artists that dream of creating the most beautiful, the most tragic, the most disturbing works, birth them here. Elites, ones that stand out among their peers while, in the background, have many secrets, hide here.

However, most of the denizens are youths. Men and women barely out of adolescents are risk-takers. Women and men with little experience hold strong optimism. They have been easily ensnared by what opportunities await them in a place where anything is possible and impossible.

That begs the question, who are you, and why have you come to Darkess Noir?

Fate is a Dish Best Served Crusted

Oswald opened his eyes as he woke from a nap. His sight was blurry with sleep. A slow blink refocused his vision to give form to the shapes in his view. A road and white boundary line zipped parallel to him. The posts of a rusted barbwire fence passed in a perfect pattern. A field of grass gradually turned in the distance. And a wall of fog, much further away, seemed to never move. He was staring out the passenger side of a car with his head resting against the window.

The cold glass felt comfortable on his forehead. He wanted to shut his eyes again and fall back to sleep. No, in actuality, he did not want that. He was looking for a way to avoid the situation.

His skin peeled off the surface as he sat up in his seat. He rubbed the spot, hoping that a mark had not been left behind. A bit of concern convinced him to flip the sun visor and check in the small mirror. His twenty-five-year-old face stared back. There was no reddening. Of course, there would not be. The only blemish was a small scar across the bridge of his nose that he always had. This was him merely delaying further.

There was no more pretending everything was alright. He turned his head slightly to the side to glance over at Jordan, who drove.

Jordan did not say anything. He continued to focus his heterochromia eyes of sea-foam-green and golden-hazel on the road. His face held contempt.

Oswald wondered if he had made a mistake. He began to move his hand toward Jordan but hesitated and withdrew. Mouth parted to speak, but words hesitated and withdrew. Eventually, eyes withdrew to the window once more. Even guilt withdrew. This was the right thing. There was no need to apologize.

7

Jordan clenched tightly onto the steering wheel. He was annoyed by what had just happened. All he wanted was an attempt to communicate. Instead, he got nothing.

He began to turn to make the needed confrontation but stopped. This was unfair. He always had to be the one that reconciled. Not this time. Head shook with disapproval as his focus returned to the road.

Ten minutes passed, accompanied by misery. The only sound was the hum of the car. Several glances went back and forth, but neither looked the other in the eye. The air in the car began to feel cold with regret. There was a bitter taste in both their mouths. This did not seem like it would end well.

Oswald saw a sign and decided to be the one to break the tension by pointing out, "Looks like there's a diner up ahead. I could eat. Hungry?"

"Fine, sure, whatever," Jordan answered dismissively.

Another five minutes of uncomfortable driving passed. They found a cliché once reaching their pitstop. The diner was an aluminum box. One large neon sign above the establishment read 'Dox Diner.'

Jordan pulled into the empty lot and parked at the closest spot. He and Oswald idly waited in their seats for words to be exchanged that might mend their feelings. Neither wanted to speak first, so neither spoke at all. After a minute, they both got out.

Oswald did not wait for his partner. He made his way immediately to the building with fast feet. He was up the four concrete steps before Jordan had locked the car, and inside before Jordan had reached the stairs.

Jordan stopped on the first step as he stared daggers through the door. His reddening face visibly showed anger. Being ignored like this was bullshit. A breath out, pluming a cloud because of the cold air, was an attempt to equalize his feelings. He entered inside with a displeased look as he stood beside Oswald.

The diner was empty of other customers and only had two employees working.

There was a waitress who appeared anywhere between sixty and eighty years of age. Wrinkles covered her skin. She had dyed-blonde hair with dark brown roots. Mascara was painted thick on her eyelids. Lips were lightly colored ruby. She wore a traditional waiting outfit that was pink in color.

A cook could be seen in the kitchen. He was a rounded black man in his forties or fifties. His skin was beading with sweat from the heat of the grill. He wore the traditional all-white outfit of a chef.

The waitress looked at the two customers and said in a gravelly voice, "Take a seat anywhere that you'd like. I'll be right with you."

"Um . . ." Oswald looked at Jordan. "Where would you like to sit?"

Jordan turned to the nearest booth. "Here's fine."

Both sat down and were opposite each other. Their seating should have forced them to look at one another. That did not happen. Oswald stared out the window while Jordan examined the diner.

The waitress approached their table, placed two menus down along with two cups of water, and upsold as she handed over one smaller menu, "Our specials for today are single-serving-pies. We have a meat pie, humble pie, mincemeat pie which does not have actual meat, not to be confused, blackberry, blueberry, cherry, apple, and rhubarb. All made fresh when you order. However, this offer is our most popular and we've already sold most. In fact, we only have enough crust for one last pie. Lucky for you if you're interested."

Oswald looked at the small menu and read the options again. "I haven't had a meat pie in a long time."

9

"Oswald?" Jordan called out in offense.

"What?" Oswald became immediately defensive.

"Do you even care at all?" Jordan sadly questioned.

"What's wrong with me getting a meat pie?" Oswald remained uncertain about what his mistake was.

"I don't eat meat," Jordan reminded that he was a vegetarian. "You know that. Did you even think that I might want something that we could share?"

"Right," Oswald rolled his eyes and scoffed.

"Don't use that tone," Jordan choked up. "This entire time you've been acting like a real asshole—"

"I'm the asshole?" Oswald barked. "You're the one that hasn't said anything."

"I've been waiting for an apology," Jordan explained.

"An apology? For what? The meat pie?" Oswald became sarcastic.

"About us driving all the way out here," Jordan made clear.

Oswald grimaced. He was not happy being reminded of what they were really fighting about. He felt he was the one being attacked suddenly. He needed to bite back. Looking at the waitress, he committed to his selfishness, "The meat pie please."

Having been witness to the argument, the waitress took a second before taking the order, her pen scribbling as she said, "right away," then she walked away.

"Unbelievable." Jordan shook his head.

Oswald ignored the verbal and non-verbal disappointments as he patted himself down. "Shit, I left my wallet in the car." He held out his hand and asked in the rudest possible way, "Keys?"

Jordan sighed as he held up the car keys.

Oswald snatched them, stood quickly, and exited the diner.

Jordan stared out the window to intently watch Oswald and wonder what was going to happen between the two of them. Both were being stubborn, one far more than the other. Both wanted to be right, one trying harder than need be.

In the kitchen, the cook looked at the ticket to see a Meat Pie Special had been ordered. An audible sigh was expelled. This was his least favorite dish to make. But he was not surprised after having heard the arguing even from back here.

He wandered across the room, opened a drawer, and pulled out the required tools for this particular preparation. Personally, he never liked the showmanship. Regardless, this was the tradition that needed to be followed else, what made the pie special would not work. So, he slipped on the elbow-long, black leather gloves. Next, a patchworked leather mask sewn together with thick black string was pulled over his head. Lastly, he gripped tightly to a crude cleaver.

Jordan fussed in his seat. He began to consider conceding during his time alone. That seemed to be the only solution to this argument. However, that would cause more problems in the long run. His own feelings constantly being put aside would make him resentful.

The kitchen door that led to the dining area swung open soundlessly. The burly beast of a butcher stepped into the room. Under the mask was hot, causing him to pant. His muffled breath sounded like a growl.

Oswald leaned in on the passenger side of the car to rummage around beneath the seat. But his blind search was unsuccessful, so he got down low to look underneath. There was nothing there. However, a colorfulness was noticed behind the seat. He got out of the front and checked the back to find his rainbow wallet laying on the floor.

The butcher slowly lumbered down the aisle as he approached the lone customer from behind. His feet dragged on the tiles creating a slight squeak with each step.

Jordan came to a decision. He would say what was on his mind. That would either end everything or be the beginning of their recovery. In either case, he would be okay with the outcome.

The butcher was halfway across the room and getting closer, and closer, and closer.

Oswald was afraid to pick up his wallet. Looking at the colorful pattern reminded him that this was a gift from his partner, a partner that he loved and cherished with all his heart. That was when he realized how stubborn he was being. Hypocritically, he had accused Jordan of not saying anything while not having spoken a word either. Jordan did not need to speak since this was not his fault. Who was to blame became obvious.

Jordan lifted his hand and made a soft fist to knock on the window to get attention. He wanted to smile and wave to let Oswald know that everything was going to be better. His wrist bent back. Chunk. His arm fell limp onto the table with a thump. A cleaver was buried into his head.

Oswald grabbed the wallet and sat in the back to look at his possession for a short time. Opening the fold found everything that a wallet was expected to have. There were also a few personal items, a small folded-up poem that read, 'My deepest wishes to you. are that your dreams come true. because you're my beau,' and a picture of them together. God, Oswald recognized himself as the asshole. Jordan must be the most amazing person to have enough patience to deal with such an unnecessarily complicated person.

The butcher stood over his kill for a second, feeling displeasure. But there was nothing he could do. The customer placed the order, and his job was to fulfill the ticket. He left the cleaver buried as he used both arms to pick up the body. The fresh meat was carried to the kitchen for preparation.

Oswald looked up at the diner with hope. He was overcome by disappointment. Jordan was gone. Things between them appeared more dire than ever.

The body was placed on top of the preparation table with a lack of finesse, making a heavy thump. The cleaver was pulled from his head, sounding sticky as thickened blood separated from the cold metal. His split open skull leaked his last thoughts onto the floor as goo.

Oswald reentered the diner with a new determination. He looked at the chosen booth hoping he would not be alone if he sat. Wishful thinking. Seeing the empty seat opposite where he would sit was not a surprise. After all, Jordan had not been there when staring in through the window.

There was only one other place Oswald expected Jordan to be. Glancing around the room found the restroom sign. That was the likely hiding spot.

The butcher stood over the body to examine where to get the meat. There was plenty to choose from. Arm raised. Cleaver chopped.

Oswald stood in front of the door to the restroom. He reached for the handle but hesitated and withdrew. Barging in would have been rude. Instead, he knocked three times.

There was no response from the other side.

"Jordan?" Oswald called out.

Just as before, there was no response.

"Jordie?" Oswald spoke with less formality to lighten the situation as he admitted, "I . . . I messed up."

The lack of response persisted, leaving a lingering melancholy that punished any continued attempts at talking.

Oswald recognized that he had truly fucked up everything. He stepped away from the door and made his way back to the booth but could not sit down. The last thing he wanted to do was have a meal alone. He remained standing as he stared out the window to collect his thoughts.

There was little he could do at this point. However, there was a selfish choice he made that he wanted to remedy. He turned toward the waitress and got her attention, "Ma'am?"

The waitress looked up from what she was doing, not bothering to smile, and wondered, "How can I help you?"

"Is it too late to ask for a humble pie instead of a meat pie?" Oswald hoped.

The waitress gave a deep frown that was somewhere in between annoyance and sympathy. "The meat is already being prepared—" she stopped to reconsider making an excuse when noticing the beaten look of the man. ". . . but I'll ask the cook." She turned toward the kitchen. "Junior?"

"Yeah?" The cook spoke in response.

"The customer is wondering if he can get a humble pie instead of a meat pie."

"Are you serious?" The cook shockingly questioned. "I've already procured the meat. There's no taking back what is done."

Oswald heard the remark and spoke up, "I'll pay the price for ordering the meat pie. Whatever the cost. But, please, I was being selfish at the time. Can you make it a humble pie?"

"You heard the young man," the waitress emphasized. "You haven't started cooking yet, have you?"

"No." The cook answered. "I was just about to lay the crust."

"Can you make the change?" She pushed the request.

There was a long pause as the cook disappointedly stared at the body. Seemed pointless to have made the kill and not use the meat for the pie. Even so, he replied with a "Fine."

The waitress turned back to Oswald, "You'll have your humble pie in a few minutes."

"Thank you," Oswald said sincerely.

He sat back down at the booth and fiddled with his phone. However, he was having difficulty doing anything on the device. His thoughts were far more distracting. Eyes kept glancing at the restroom. He kept waiting and wanting Jordan to come out.

Clank. Oswald was startled by the sound. He looked down to see a pie set in front of him. His attention had been so sidetracked that he had not noticed the waitress approach until she placed the plate on the table.

"Here you go, Hun," she said with a bent yet well-intentioned smile unlike before.

The humble pie was an outstandingly perfect-looking pastry. The top had been baked to the most beautiful golden brown. Pressing a fork into the crust felt satisfying with how flaky the dish was. Steam rose as the sweet smell of cooked sugar burst forth. A vibrant colored jelly filling, made from an assortment of berries and peaches, spilled out.

Oswald became seduced. Inhaling the aroma had his eyes rolling to the back of his head. He licked his lips. His stomach gluttonously grumbled. But something was wrong. He could not take a bite.

He stood up with the pie and went to the restroom. Knock, knock. "Jordie? Please come out. I don't want to talk through the door. We should be face to face."

Nothing.

Oswald felt as if he truly brought ruin to their relationship. He hoped his expression of regret was enough to fix what he had done. "I asked them to change the order. I've got a humble pie. I want to share it with you."

Nothing.

Oswald was completely defeated at this point. He went back to his seat. The pie was meant to be his apology. Now it was his comfort. He began to eat. Fork scooped a piece into his mouth. The taste on his tongue was like no other. Too delicious to deny and too sad to have self-restraint, he ate it all.

The empty dish sat coldly in front of him. Now there was nothing left to offer relief from his growing sadness. He buried his face in his hands. A knot in his throat was swallowed. He wanted to cry, but tears were held back.

The waitress approached to ask, "How was the pie?"

"Good," Oswald was able to answer with some composure. "Thanks for making the change."

"You're very welcome," the waitress accepted the gratitude. Her expression turned serious. "Is there a point in your life that you wish to go back and change? Something you realized you were at fault for and wanted to accept responsibility for? A chance to be humble?"

"Yeah," Oswald answered, the word a breath. "I'm not surprised you're asking. We've made it clear that things aren't going well between us. It's my fault, of course. I just didn't want to be blamed for putting us here. I wish I could go back to the car ride and say something."

"Pay when you're ready, Sir." The waitress placed the bill on the table.

Oswald handed his debit card over before the waitress walked away.

She took the plastic and went straight to the cash register. Swipe.

Oswald opened his eyes as he woke from a nap. His sight was blurry with sleep. A slow blink refocused his vision to give form to the shapes in his view. A road and white boundary line zipped parallel to him. The posts of a rusted barbwire fence passed in a perfect pattern. A field of grass gradually turned in the distance. And a wall of fog, much further away, seemed to never move. He was staring out the passenger side of a car with his head resting against the window.

The cold glass felt comfortable on his forehead. He wanted to shut his eyes again and fall back to sleep. No, in actuality, he did not want that. He was looking for a way to avoid the situation.

His skin peeled off the surface as he sat up in his seat. He rubbed the spot, hoping that a mark had not been left behind. A bit of concern convinced him to flip the sun visor and check in the small mirror. His twenty-five-year-old face stared back. There was no reddening. Of course, there would not be. The only blemish was a small scar across the bridge of his nose that he always had. This was him merely delaying further.

There was no more pretending everything was alright. He turned his head slightly to the side to glance over at Jordan, who drove.

Jordan did not say anything. He continued to focus his heterochromia eyes of sea-foam-green and golden-hazel on the road. His face held contempt.

Oswald wondered if he had made a mistake. He began to move his hand toward Jordan but hesitated and . . . there was no withdrawing. Oswald reached all the way forward, taking hold of Jordan's hand.

Jordan twitched with surprise then became more relaxed than before. He took a breath finding peace as his face appeared ready to cry with tears of happiness. His fingers curled tightly to hold onto Oswald.

"I'm sorry," Oswald admitted. "I think I ruined your life. You quit your job. You had to leave your family behind. You uprooted everything for me so that we could move out here to a place that you never wanted to be. Coming here is only for my sake, for a career opportunity, something that doesn't affect you. You would've had a perfect life had you stayed. But you still came.

"Instead of appreciating the sacrifices you've made, I've resented you. I've felt that you must hate me for what I've done. I've tried to convince you how much better your life will be as long as you listen to what I say. But I realize now that that's just me trying to control you. And now you've become distant. And I know that I'm the one to blame. But I've been using that as an excuse to blame you for everything instead. I'm sorry. I'm so fucking sorry. You deserve better."

Jordan was moved by the admission. A tear fell from his eye. He took a breath to find the words he wanted to respond with and started slow, "Thank you. I could feel the pressure you kept putting on me. You've been constantly trying to convince me that everything I'm leaving behind doesn't matter. But it does. So, don't tell me my life is going to be better. Trying to minimize my life feels so disrespectful as if I'm not important. I should be the most important person to you.

"And let me be sad. You wouldn't let me be sad. You're acting like my sadness makes you the bad guy. You weren't the bad guy until that started. You're supposed to comfort me in my time of need, not pretend everything is alright. I'm hurt, Oswald. Not by you at first. Just grieving like a normal person. Then I was hurting only because of you. Please stop telling me what's good for me. I decide that. Treat me like I matter, like you care about me. Stop protecting yourself instead of protecting this relationship, please. Please, Oswald. Please."

Oswald was covering his face. Little did that help. Many tears were running down his cheeks. "I've been acting like a selfish child. I don't want to lose you but you being sad felt like I was losing you. I couldn't bear being responsible for your pain. I thought devaluing what you had would make you glad to come with me, that what I offered was better. I understand how wrong I've been. Your past and where you come from will always be a part of you. All I've been doing is treating your life as a cancer that needed to be cut out. But I'm the cancer trying to destroy you from the inside. How could you ever forgive me?"

Jordan squeezed Oswald's hand tightly. "You're being honest with me. I can forgive that. I forgive you."

"Why?" Oswald was dumbfounded.

Jordan smiled to assure that everything was alright as he explained, "I love you, Oswald. Don't think you're ruining my life. I came with you because I wanted to. If I didn't want to be here, I wouldn't have left. This was my decision that you, in no way, influenced."

Oswald lightly exhaled out his nose as a pathetic laugh knowing that was untrue but finding the claim humorous.

"Well, okay, me moving had everything to do with you," Jordan corrected, "but I'm here for you, not because of you."

"Jordie?" Oswald called.

Jordan smiled widely, hearing his nickname. "Yes?"

"I love you."

Jordan had many small reactions of joy. Those were the three words that mattered. And he felt the same way, "I love you, too."

Oswald leaned in closer. Jordan stared at the road to make sure there were no hazards before turning his head. The two lightly kissed as proof everything would be alright.

The mood in the car was heavyhearted yet filled with relief. Oswald leaned back in his seat to relax. Jordan turned on the radio adding the sound of soft rock to their drive. The two would glance back and forth, catch each other's eyes, and smile. There was a warmness between them once again. Their relationship was beginning to heal.

A sign came into view, and Jordan spoke up, "Hey. There's a diner. How do you feel about getting something to eat?"

Oswald considered his appetite and realized, "Surprisingly, I'm not that hungry. But I'd like to stop anyways. After our talk, I could use a chance to stretch my legs."

"I'll massage them tonight," Jordan offered before agreeing with Oswald, "And we can take a rest now."

Five minutes of driving passed quickly. Their light chatting kept the awkwardness away. Of course, some anxieties remained. That did not prevent them from being happy.

When they were close to their stop, the signage visible enough to see, Oswald read the name aloud, "Dox Diner. Looks exactly like every other diner."

"All diners are familiar. That's what makes these places comfortable," Jordan suggested as he pulled into the empty lot and parked at the closest spot.

"Maybe too familiar," Oswald said with unease. "I'm having serious Déjà vu. I feel like we've been here before."

"You know what? I feel the same," Jordan agreed. However, he was excited by the odd recollection. "Let's go in. I want to see if I keep feeling the same once we're inside."

"Uh . . ." Oswald was less thrilled but accepted, "after you."

Both got out of the car, made their way up the four concrete steps, and entered the building. The diner was empty of other customers and only had two employees working, an old waitress and a black cook. This place and these people were as recognizable as a word trapped on the tip of the tongue, or a memory that could not quite be placed. That false certainty was unsettling.

Oswald shuttered as a chill ran down his spine. He wanted to leave.

Jordan held a curious interest. He turned to the nearest booth. The seats were unoccupied but only recently. Remaining on the table were two menus, a small menu, a couple of cups of water, and an empty plate covered in flakes of piecrust with a used fork resting on the dish. He moved closer to the mess and picked up the small menu to look over the options.

One of the specials stood out to Jordan, "They serve meat pies here. Those are your favorite. When's the last time you had one?"

Oswald took position just over Jordan's shoulder to look at the menu and remarked, "It's been a while. Not since the last time my mom sent me one. But you're a vegetarian; we should get something that we both can enjoy. Plus, I'm not that hungry."

"Maybe we get one to go?" Jordan suggested.

"Maybe?" Oswald considered.

The waitress approached, interrupting the discussion.

Oswald and Jordan became silent and stared.

She explained, "We're not serving anymore of our specials today. We just used up all the piecrust." Her eyes looked directly at Oswald. "Hopefully, our last customer is satisfied with his humble pie."

Oswald tilted his head to the side with puzzlement. There was something he seemed to be forgetting. Then he began to notice a trace of sweetness lingering on his taste buds.

"Now then," the waitress redirected, "we do have an abundance of fresh meat, recently procured, so prices are lowered."

"Thanks for letting us know," Oswald appreciated but knew he had no interest in the offer.

"I don't eat meat," Jordan gave as his excuse, which was not a lie. However, he also had a disturbing feeling that he could not shake. Looking toward the kitchen, watching the cook through the small window hacking away at something just out of sight, there was a sickening feeling as if the cleaver was cutting into his own flesh.

"We do still have plenty of options for you," the waitress assured. "Go ahead and take a seat anywhere that you'd like. Look over the menu. I'll be right with you in a moment."

"Uhm?" Oswald held up his hand to stop her from going. He had something important to ask.

22

"What do you need?" She obliged.

"Do you know how much further down the road we need to go until we reach Darkess Noir?" That was their destination.

"You're in Darkess, Hun," she informed. "Arrived about a mile back."

"Really?"

Oswald and Jordan turned to look out the window out of curiosity. What they saw brought them unease, and goosebumps were quick to cover their skin. A thick fog blanketed over the world.

"When did that roll in?"

Mansion in the Rain

Within the boundary of Darkess Noir was a paved parkway named Rabbit-Hollow Road. Forestry flourished thick on both sides, making the route rather shady on a normal day. But now was night, and rain fell heavily. Visibility had completely vanished.

A dark-blue minivan, color melding with the surroundings, drove the road at a cautious speed. Wipers tried to keep the windshield clear to little effect. The downpour had become so bad that water endlessly cascaded over the front of the car. The headlights could no longer cut through the thick darkness that was ahead. The driver, Martha, a mature woman, tried to see what was in front of her by leaning forward over the steering wheel. Her trick did not help much. In the end, she slowed to a stop, parked on the side of the road, and turned the hazards on. It would be too dangerous to continue forward.

In the car with Martha was her husband, Adam, and their teenage son, Ben. The three of them were worried about this predicament. They needed to be in the city by morning. As the coordinators of a rally that would be taking place the next day by midday, they needed time to make final preparations as well as have a little bit of rest.

"Are we lost?" Ben asked, unsure as to why they had stopped.

"There's only one road to follow," Adam replied. "All we have to do is go straight."

"Easier said than done," Martha asserted. "Driving in this weather is impossible, regardless that there is only the one road. We'll keep going when this storm eases up."

"Just be slow," Adam snidely explained.

"Yeah," Martha began sarcastically, "that'll work until a car comes up from behind and crashes into us."

"Anybody else on this road will also be driving slow," Adam assumed.

"And what if they're not?" Martha challenged.

As parents bickered, Ben let his mind wander since there was nothing that he could contribute to the argument. As he idly began staring into the storm, something obvious stood out in the surrounding bleak blackness. He became vocal about his discovery, "What's that?"

"What are you talking about?" Adam wondered in response to abruptly break away from his other conversation. Looking quickly spied the same phenomena.

Martha did not bother being upset with her husband's change of topic. Instead, she took the opportunity to gander herself. Eyes caught sight of the same thing the other two had seen.

Straight in front, floating in the air, was a rectangle of burning orange light. That could not possibly be from a car. The size was too big. The placement was too high up. It had to be coming from a second or third story window of some house.

Martha turned the ignition.

"What are you doing?" Adam objected to the presumed action.

"Getting closer," Martha explained. She began driving the car before there could be any more protest.

Once only a few feet forward, shades of night thinned, and the blurred silhouette of a mansion appeared not that far ahead. Simple architecture of windows, pillars, and balconies was discernible. However, the size was impossible to determine. Other than the very front of the building, higher up stories and the sides were faded from sight.

"How did we get here?" Ben asked. "I thought this road went directly to Darkess Noir?"

"There are a few side roads leading to rich people's homes," Adam made an assumption. "With the weather so bad, your mother must have driven down one by mistake."

"Good thing," Ben recognized the silver lining. "Think if we ask politely, the owner might let us stay for the night?"

"We need to get to the city by tonight," Adam stressed.

"Well," Martha contradicted, "not really. We need a place to stay for the night. If we stay here, we can get the important tasks done, then leave early in the morning to begin the rally on time."

"So, you think we should just beg for a place to stay?" Adam disapproved of being so humble.

"Not beg." Martha rolled her eyes. "Ask for help. It's a terrible night. No way the storm is going to let up. Thinking so is just wishful. Better that we put down our pride so we can better bring attention to the real issues tomorrow."

"Fine," Adam conceded.

Martha had a winning smile.

Moving the car again, they parked as close to the front entrance as possible which happened to be at the bottom of a wide stairway. Each family member gathered their important things first, then together, they rushed out of the car to the front door. Under the archway of the entrance was safe from the rain. Unfortunately, what short time they spent in the torrent had left them completely drenched. Now there was no going back on this decision. They needed a warm place to dry.

The bell was pressed, and four resounding gongs echoed. After a moment of waiting, the door opened. Inside stood a handsome, Victorian man.

"How may I help you?" The man questioned.

"We hate to ask," Martha spoke, hopeful, "but we got caught in this storm. The roads are too unsafe to drive. So, we were wondering if we could stay the night?"

"I cannot leave you to bear these terrible elements," the man spoke sympathetically. Truly, the expression on his face showed how much he cared. That made his following words, words that were so filled with an unknown melancholy, deeply concerning, "You are welcome to come in."

"Thank you," Martha appreciated for her whole family.

"Don't," the man knew there was no gratitude to be felt toward him. He turned away and began into the depths of his home, the shadows consuming his presence. His final offering resounded from all around, "Have a goodnight."

"What a freak," Adam said under his breath.

Nobody disputed that fact.

The family did not take long to begin exploring the mansion.

Martha first found her way to a bedroom. Her wet clothing left her feeling uncomfortable, and she needed to change. Luckily, a provided robe offered her such a chance. Once redressed, she searched around for the kitchen and began making meals for herself and her two boys.

Adam decided to take full advantage of the hospitality with a long bath. Steam filled the room like a sauna. He became so relaxed in the warm water after having been drenched by the cold rain that he fell into a nap.

Ben, as most daring men his age do, looked for cool things. There was a suit of armor he found to his liking in the foyer, but it did not hold his interest for long. Seeking further entertainment had him happen upon a

27

trophy room filled with stuffed and mounted beasts. Certainly, he was distracted for longer, but eventually his curiosity faded. The next room to draw him in held a remarkable gun collection. That, too, became a passing fancy. The library was the last room he found. Not a place he would normally investigate, but he took the time to look around, thinking that there could be some amusing books.

So many shelves were lined with so many titles that ranged from poetry to epics to encyclopedias, none of which caught Ben's attention. Instead, the least interesting, most plain, easily overlooked book drew him in, and he tried to pull the hardcover from its spot. But it did not completely come free. Instead, there was a click, and gears could be heard whirring. The shelf swung back, revealing a secret passage. On the other side was a spiral staircase descending to a lower floor.

Ben had found a new interest and began down the steps. Hanging lanterns lit the way, the flames of which flickered often due to a constant cold draft. The rush of air seemed to be attempting to push the boy back the way he came. But he did not care to turn around. Not even the disturbing claw marks etched deep in the stone walls were warning enough. He continued until he reached the bottom where there was another door.

He entered with no fear, but he was not acting out of bravery. The basement room was cold and cryptic. Cobwebs filled the corners. A single candle sat on a wooden desk that was placed up against the right wall. On the left hung a clock, ticking away the time. However, the most prominent adornment was an iron cage in the center. Sealed inside was the Victorian man, lying on a humble bed.

Ben approached with curiosity. After taking a moment to stare as if looking into the pen at a zoo, he called out, "Hello?"

There was no reaction.

Not receiving a reply immediately caused Ben to become disinterested. Looking around for some new excitement, he noticed a key hanging on a hook next to the door. He had an idea what the key was for and chose to find out if he was right for no other reason than boredom. The door to the cage unlocked with a click and swung open freely.

"You shouldn't have come down here," the Victorina man warned too late. Though, him having been awake the entire time was a sign that he had been waiting and expecting this to happen.

The clock struck midnight. The man was suddenly standing. A series of chimes rang a recognizable melody followed by low gongs resonating the time. Gong! He hunched over in pain. Gong! His body wrenched again. Gong! His spine and shoulders jutted. Gong! Fingers and hands began to elongate, nails becoming sharp. Gong! Legs deformed into something resembling a dog. Gong! Hair began to sprout from every pore. Gong! Cries of pain turned into a deep growl. Gong! Ears became pointed. Gong! Eyes turned a ferocious yellow. Gong! Teeth were sharp. Gong! Face began stretching into a muzzle. On the final Gong! the transformation was complete, and the beast howled.

Ben had been paralyzed by fright the moment the clock had begun to ring. Wide eyes could not look away from what was happening directly before him. Only thoughts of terrifying wonder raced through his mind. Running away was not even considered. Regardless, had such a thought occurred, his legs shook so badly that taking a step would have him fall to the ground immediately. There was no chance to escape.

The beast turned to the prey. A leap as sudden as lightning crossed the distance between the two. Teeth dug into the soft flesh of the throat.

29

Adam woke from his nap when the clock struck midnight and finished his bath shortly after the final stroke. As he stood in front of the fogged mirror, he could see nothing in the reflection. With a hand towel, he wiped away some of the condensation. Revealed behind him, to his fright, was a heinous beast. Such a thing was too unbelievable. Turning around was all he could do to make sure his mind was not playing tricks. He screamed out when the reality was revealed. A claw ripped across his chest.

Martha waited in the dining room for her husband and son. However, they were taking their time with whatever distractions they had found. She tried to message them via text. Unfortunately, there was no signal in the mansion. That left her resigned to wait. But, as time stretched to concerning lengths, her worry grew.

What concerns she had faded as the sound of footsteps could be heard approaching the room. She looked toward the entryway where the steps would come to be. Standing in the shadows was the silhouette of some large animal. She did not hesitate to get up from her seat and run.

The beast charged after her, leaping onto the table, and tearing across.

She reached the entryway on the other side of the room.

The beast leaped with claws extended.

Turning the corner barely escaped and she continued to run through the halls looking for the front entrance.

The beast hit the ground unexpectedly, causing it to slide forward and crash into furniture. The smash left it jumbled for a moment. Getting back on its feet and shaking fur, the hunt began again.

As Martha ran, she attempted to call the police only to remember she had no signal. So afraid and frustrated, she was not looking where she was going. Her feet caught on a rug, and she tripped. While on the ground, she looked back over her shoulder. The beast was nowhere to be seen. That gave her a small relief. She got back up and continued to make her escape. Fortunately, the room at the end of the hall was the foyer.

Bursting through the front door put her outside. Heavy rain had yet to cease. She ran down the wet steps, almost tripping again, and got to her car. Eyes darted around as she fumbled with her keys. They dropped out of her hand. She cursed out, "Shit!" and scrambled to pick them back up. Once retrieved, she had no problems finding the car key and unlocking the door. Inside felt safe. But getting away would feel much safer. She tried to start the engine. It refused. "Come on!" she begged. The cylinders sputtered weakly. "God damn it!" The vehicle was never going to work.

The door was suddenly ripped off. She screamed. Her cry was quick to be silenced as she was pulled out and torn apart.

Though the moon still sat in the sky so brightly, the Victorian man transformed back into his human form. The catalyst was never the satellite that floated overhead. It was the three people. Now that they were dead, remaining the beast was pointless.

He reentered his mansion, naked, soaked from head to toe, still dripping with the blood of those he killed. From the many doors the foyer had, along with several secret passages hidden in the staircase and behind false walls, dozens of scientist-technician types entered the room.

"Lord Arlo," the supervisor of the rest spoke to the Victorian man with praise, "another wonderful encounter."

"If you say so," Lord Arlo cared not.

Within the walls of Arlo Manor resided a man known to the world as Lord Arlo. He was no more than a monster wearing human skin as clothing. Through a window he watched the world pass by, day by day, waiting for the day he had to work. They were far and few in between, which was a blessing, for work he feared the most. Yet, a day would come when his work beckoned.

The days of work always occurred on the darkest of nights, during the heaviest of rains, or days of thickest fogs. Always, a stranger or strangers would become lost, fall into trouble, or simply need a place to shelter away from the ominous. They would find their way to his mansion that was so well hidden in the depths of Darkess Noir. Their fate was sealed the moment they knocked upon his door and asked to enter.

Lord Arlo had to always allow entry to those that came to his home, whether they be a single person or a large group, a naïve individual or a violent criminal. They always explored the mansion, noticing the valuables that piqued their interest. However, with closer inspection, they always discovered the many oddities concealed by the lavish lifestyle. Then they would trigger the encounter resulting in their demise, in one way or another.

There was an impenetrable fog today.

The researchers stood around the mansion, going over their data. Some examined the outcomes of previous encounters. Others were busy planning new encounters.

Lord Arlo sat in his study. A fireplace popped and crackled in front of him. A book on his lap had been acting as an enjoyable diversion. At the moment, however, he had become distracted by a distressful feeling. Now his eyes were focused on the window.

A researcher entered the room, announcing, "We have another pair of guests. Shall we begin?"

"If we must." Lord Arlo was disappointed.

"What should we do for today's encounter?" The researcher offered a chance to make a choice. "Death Traps? Possessed Doll? Vampire?"

"I don't care," Lord Arlo just wanted to be over and done with this bloody mess.

"This fog is too thick," Jordan declared as he brought the car to a stop. He sighed at the unfortunate circumstance. However, a smile crossed his face, and his heterochromia eyes of sea-foam-green and golden-hazel lit up; the situation did not have to be like that. He unbuckled himself from his seat, plopped down on Oswald's lap, wrapped arms around Oswald's neck, and remarked, "We're not going anywhere, anytime soon. What should we do?"

Oswald got the hint and began nuzzling his nose, with the small scar across the bridge, against Jordan's neck. That was the sweet spot that evoked a choir of soft moans. Two young men, lost in love, hidden in a haze, could get away with just about anything. That was if they were truly alone.

Oswald checked around to make sure they did have privacy. To his dismay, he spied a curiosity proving otherwise. Straight in front, floating in the air, was a rectangle of burning orange light. No doubt it was a light from the window of some house.

33

"I think someone's home is right there?" Oswald mentioned, ruining the mood.

Jordan looked and was displeased. Then he gave a clumsy smile, "Think we should give them a show?"

"No," Oswald did not hesitate.

Jordan smilingly sighed. That was the expected answer. So, he suggested, "Do you want to go check it out?"

"No," Oswald did not care but did have a humorous tone instead of something akin to negativity.

"Well," Jordan pressured, "you got to choose one."

"You choose," Oswald toyed.

"You know I can't," Jordan smile frowned. "I'm bad at making decisions. I gave you the two options. It's your turn to narrow it down to one."

Oswald kissed Jordan on the cheek and then said, "Let's go see what's there."

Jordan smilingly sighed again. What a tease. But that was the expected answer.

The two got out of the car and made their way toward what beckoned.

Before the great oak door, Oswald stood a bit further back on the top step, and Jordan stood closest so he could push the doorbell. Four resounding gongs echoed. Then they waited.

Oswald said with skepticism, "Do you really think a person that lives in this kind of mansion would like strangers stopping by?"

"Who knows?" Jordan did not mind being intrusive.

The door creaked open. Inside stood a handsome, Victorian man, Lord Arlo.

"We're sorry to bother you," Jordan played up the charm. "The fog is really thick. We kind of got lost."

"It's quite alright," Lord Arlo was sympathetic. "Are you looking for shelter?"

"Not so much," Oswald answered truthfully. "This one," pointing at Jordan, "is acting like a lost puppy, but he really just wants to explore."

"Oswald!" Jordan gave a genuinely offended look like he had been snitched on. Hands soundlessly clapped together as eyes shut to rebalance himself. He forgave immediately, remembering Oswald was blunt, honest, and tended to not recognize the importance of small secrets. Admittance followed, "You know I love the fog."

Lord Arlo looked at Oswald intently.

Jordan noticed the look and he became jealous. "I hope you're not getting any ideas."

"You two are . . ." Lord Arlo was caught off guard. "Sorry. I'm not . . ." He took a breath feeling flustered for the first time in a long time. A moment of pause was taken before he demanded, "Leave."

"What?" Jordan felt so insulted he needed to hear what had been said again.

"You are not welcome in my home," Lord Arlo affirmed.

"Do you have a problem with our relationship?" Jordan assumed the worst.

"If I say yes, will you leave?" Lord Arlo tested.

"You—" Jordan was about to go off.

"Let's go," Oswald diffused the situation with the simple declaration.

Jordan continued to stand at the ready, wanting a fight.

Oswald reached forward and held out his hand beside Jordan.

Jordan took the offering and became calmish.

Both left.

Jordan stormed across the courtyard with balled fists, not saying a word. Oswald stayed close behind, more concerned with Jordan's feelings than caring about the unpleasant experience. Both got back to the car and got in. Silence lingered as they sat completely still in their seats.

Oswald knew that there were moments to talk and moments not to. Speaking right now would only have anger thrown his way. But he knew how to reach out without that risk. Just as before, when they stood before the door, he held out his hand.

Jordan glared at the offering. Not because he was mad with it. His anger was elsewhere. Unfortunately, whatever he stared at, incidentally, took a scolding. He accepted the comfort by aggressively grabbing hold and then turned to stare out the window.

Oswald grimaced as his hand was squeezed tight by feelings of frustration. He was well aware the anger was not directed at him. And he did not mind in the least having to deal with the residual emotions.

"I cannot believe there are still people like that," Jordan voiced allowed, though mainly to himself. His head shook slightly with disbelief.

"There will always be people like that," Oswald remarked. "Just ignore them. They don't matter."

"How come you're not pissed off right now?" Jordan began to turn against Oswald for acting so passive.

"They don't matter," Oswald reiterated. "If I got mad at them, I'd just be giving them power over me."

"So, you're saying I'm giving that guy power over me?" Jordan was building to an argument.

"Yes," Oswald admitted. This was why he did not want to speak. Now anger was going to be projected at him, but that was his point, "You're angry at me even though I'm on your side. That guy is an asshole. I do hate him because he's ignorant. He doesn't understand what it's like to be us. Better to say, we aren't like him. That makes us different. And what's different in his eyes must be wrong in some way. But really, he's closed off from the world, and all he's doing with that hate is dragging people like us into his terrible world. I want you to be happy with me, right now, instead of lost in your head, angry at a person that will never change. Just forget that guy, or else he wins."

"That's . . ." The revulsion of that man was like a toxin. Jordan realized he had been infected and his own hate was beginning to poison his relationship. The best thing would be to forgive and forget so that his life would not be paused by this meaningless interaction. Forgetting would be easy enough, and forgiving would not be necessary once he forgot. He finished his statement with an insincere, "stupid," mumbled between pursed lips.

Oswald kissed Jordan on the hand to accept the apology, then said, "You don't need to be over it right away. You're allowed to feel how you feel. But—"

"Don't take it out on you," Jordan assumed.

"I'm okay taking your anger," Oswald admitted with a smile. "Whatever you need to do to feel better. But—"

"You're stupid," Jordan remarked in a playful way.

"That's true," Oswald accepted the fun-loving bullying. "But . . ." a short pause followed to make sure there was not a third interruption, "never mind."

"Come on," Jordan coaxed. After such suspense, now he wanted to know what was next.

37

"Well. . . after having the time to think about what I planned to say, it feels stupid now. Instead, I'll just say I love you."

"I love you, too," Jordan said back. His anger was mostly gone, his happiness returning, and his curiosity peaked at the moment, "Why has this road trip been so emotional?"

"What was your astrological sign again?" Oswald jokingly brought up as a way to imply that could be the reason.

"Shut up." Jordan smirked. "You're no better. Now, the fog has lifted enough. Let's find our new home."

After Lord Arlo shut the front entrance, the researchers appeared from the many doors and secret passages. Every one of them had a concerned looked.

One approached, stating, "Lord Arlo? What about the encounter? The administrators will not be please."

"Let them be upset," Lord Arlo cared not and wandered to another room. He was followed by the gaggle. "Let it be known that those two are not victims. I, Francis Arlo, declare them to be family of Darkess Noir."

As he made this announcement, he looked upon a painting of a glorious woman. She was a friend of his from centuries past. The first and only woman he loved. Unfortunately, they could never be together for he was a monster and she a human, though more like a Divine Goddess in his eyes. Madam Rook was the founder of this dreamscape city. And, having studied her face so intently, for so many years, the resemblance was unquestionable. That man by the name of Oswald was a part of her bloodline.

Beast Fiend

Cellphone rang and buzzed, slowly vibrating across the nightstand. Travis woke to the familiar sound, and his hand instinctively grabbed the device. Pressing the home button, the screen lit up with a bright and blinding light, forcing him to squint his eyes. He first looked at the time, three o'clock, before seeing the 'who' that would be calling this late. But the number was just that, a string of numbers not saved to his contacts. He hung up. If the call was important, they would call again or leave a voicemail.

Head buried back into his pillow. Having been barely awakened, he was already in the first stages of slumber and eager to return. But he did not get the chance. His phone rang again.

This time, he grabbed his phone and brought it directly to his ear, not bothering to look at the screen. His voice was groggy when he answered the call with a question, "Hello?"

"Is this Mr. Polt?" A woman on the other end of the line asked.

"Yes," Travis kept dialogue short. "Who's this?"

"I'm calling on behalf of St. Kindred Hospital," she explained. "I'm sorry to inform you that your sister was involved in an accident, rushed to the hospital, and . . ." a short pause to delay revealing the reality of the situation felt like forever. Eventually, the word had to be said, "died."

At this point, Travis was sitting up in his bed, fully awake. He did not know what emotion to express. He did not even know what to say. So, he asked, "What should I do?"

"Please, come to the facility," she instructed. "There's paperwork that needs to be signed." Then her

39

professional façade was dropped, "I know this is hard to hear. And it will be harder to face. But you should be here to say your goodbyes."

That felt too late, but Travis knew what the woman meant. "I'll head right over. Has our mom been told?"

"Yes."

"Thank you." He hung up quickly after, afraid to stay on the line, unsure what else could be revealed.

Travis stood outside his front door with an expression of uncertainty. He looked down. At his side, there sat a curious dog, a beagle, head slightly cocked and tail slowly wagging. His sister had given him custody of her dog, Killian, after she had passed away.

The dog was cute; there was no doubt about that. But Travis did not really like that this responsibility was thrust upon him. Now his life would be scheduled around taking care of something he never wanted.

Regardless of how the situation made him feel, he opened the door for his new pet.

Travis soon discovered several issues that quickly began to ruin his life.

He was ruled by the tediousness of taking care of a dog. Three walks had to be done day in and day out, like clockwork, the same time, the same route, the same pees and poops, over and over. This constant cycle dominated his schedule, destroyed his free time. He could not stay out anywhere overnight without someone to take care of the dog. Life lost the spontaneous excitement, rarely occurring or not, and became endlessly predictable. Everything soon melded into one another. And his resentment grew and grew.

Then there were the added expenses of food and vet visits. The need to feed would not usually be that much of an issue when buying for a normal dog. A fifty-pound bag of food could be purchased for ten dollars. Unfortunately, such a cheap product was made with cheap ingredients, mainly wheat or rice. Killian was discovered to have a grain allergy and could not eat the basic name brands sold at every store without him being struck by auto-cannibalism. Instead, Travis had to buy the smaller and far more expensive fifty-dollar bags of food. And Killian needed to be flea-treated. And Killian needed to take pills for a bacterial build-up that was causing bloody diarrhea. And Killian had hip dysplasia. And Killian, Killian, Killian cost more and more and more.

Time and finances were a reasonable trade any owner would make for a pet that they loved. But Travis did not love Killian. He was annoyed by the dog and his annoyance steadily built day by day.

The howling was annoying. And there was so much howling. Leaving the room for a moment, Killian would howl. If there was another dog, Killian would howl. Seeing a person, Killian would howl. Travis found this irritating enough in his home. At least he lived without roommates and the walls were thick enough that the neighbors did not complain. Regardless, just the fact that this disturbance existed was a bother to him. But the real issue was when howling at others. Dogs barked back, upsetting the owners. People became standoffish, regardless that Killian was small. Travis was left feeling embarrassed.

Then there was the digging. The digging was the worst. Every day, everywhere, Killian would dig and dig and dig. In the backyard. On the trails in the park. On other people's lawns. Travis was pissed that his backyard was being ruined. He felt anxious about the endless holes in the park because he did not want to be blamed for the damage or potential risk they posed. And he hated the blame he did get about the holes in other people's lawns. He was under constant growing stress. Those holes. Those holes. Why so many damn holes? They were endless. Deep. If Travis took his eyes off Killian for a moment, as soon as he looked back, there would be a hole at least a foot deep. Sniff, sniff, dig voraciously.

Unable to handle the situation, not even really knowing how to handle everything that was piling on, Travis started by yelling. His voice would tear at terrible volumes, berating with cruel words. Killian only understood the tone, and that was enough to frighten him. He would slump with his tail between his legs and avoid eye contact. But that fixed nothing.

Then the hitting began. It started with a bop on the head and, when only mildly annoyed, would remain no more than a bop. As tension grew, however, Travis would seriously slap Killian across the muzzle. Further aggravation resulted in a pin to the ground, as if some display of dominance, and a vicious whisper of further threats of violence. But the bursts of spontaneous rage were the worse. Travis had kicked, thrown, shaken, and once hurled a remote at the dog. Killian cowered from the abuse. But that fixed nothing. The howling and digging would always start up again.

Soon, Travis had given up completely.

He stood outside, a plastic bag of poop in one hand, leash in the other, as he stared dead-eyed at the dog who was digging a hole. Standing next to him was the neighbor lady badgering on and on about how the dog kept digging holes in her yard, that Travis needed to take responsibility, that Travis needed to learn to take control of his pet. In honesty, he had zoned her out. This was not the first lecture and would not be the last. Killian would never stop. And, in turn, neither would the annoying complaints.

"Are you listening to me!?" The lady shouted for attention.

The volume was loud enough to register a reaction, though Travis responded as dismissively as he had been acting. "Not really?"

She threatened, "If you don't train your dog, I'll have him taken away."

"Good," Travis openly admitted. That idea sounded just fine.

Such a response offended the lady. She disappointingly shook her head. "If you don't want him, then why don't you take him to the pound?"

Travis did then immediately wonder why he had not gotten rid of Killian. He did not care for the dog. It was a source of constant burden. The truth he realized was that his pride kept him from doing so. His deceased sister had given him this responsibility. To just do away with Killian would upset their mom, his friends, and his sister's friends, all of whom had cheered him on for such selflessness. He did not want to be shamed by going back on what he had promised.

But if this neighbor lady had the dog taken away, it would not be his fault. The blame could be put on someone else. Such a thought brought a delightful smile.

That selfish hope never happened. There were constant complaints directed at him that drove him mad, but nobody seemed to want to report him. In fact, he began to fear being reported. So many people could corroborate that he was a poor owner, and he would receive the blame and be judged. Something needed to change.

The night was late. Travis sat in his living room, television on, though the screen received little love. He

43

stared devilishly at the dog which barked and howled at the sliding, glass backdoor.

Tonight was darker than most. Not only was the wall of fog thicker, but heavy clouds also covered the sky trapping the city. There would be little visibility. Only the desperate and suspicious would be out. A perfect chance to be one of them.

Travis stood, put Killian on a leash, and they left for a walk. Block by block, the small suburb was navigated. Killian would attempt to stop for a pee or dig a hole. That led to Travis harshly yanking the leash and dragging the dog along. He did not care to care any longer.

Eventually, they reached a tree line. Nothing other than creeping shadows waited within. Such nightmares would not detour Travis. They entered the woods. Deeper and deeper they went, leaving civilization behind.

A spot of no importance was decided upon. Travis let Killian off the leash. Soon, the dog did as expected. He dug and dug and dug. He dug for so long. He dug so far down that, by the time he was too exhausted to dig anymore, he realized he was in a hole too deep for him to jump out of. He tried and tried to get out but to no avail. His desperate yapping called for help.

Travis saw this as a fitting end. If the dog was not going to stop being a problem, then let the problem be the demise. Travis shoved the dirt pile back into the hole. Killian was suddenly buried beneath the avalanche, still alive. Those desperate yaps echoed out two more times from beneath the ground before being brought to silence by the suffocating earth.

Travis used his foot to gradually push more of the dirt over the hole to make sure nothing would be crawling out. The problem was solved. He felt content and began his return home.

Travis tossed his keys lazily on an end table by the front door when he returned. Hands attempted to wipe tiredness away from his face. Little did that help. He yawned deeply. The buildup of stress over these weeks accompanied by the late-night affair had him ready for a peaceful rest.

He went upstairs to his bedroom. He showered first to clean off the grime of everything that happened. Then the covers called, comfortably cradling him to sleep.

Darkness took over quickly. There were no seconds used for thought beforehand. There were no dreams that followed. He was just out in an instant, deeply asleep. But sleep did not last long. Yap!

Travis snapped open his eyes to the sound that he did not remember the sound of. He took a moment to listen carefully. There was nothing. Must have been his imagination. So, his eyes shut again.

Though there was no reoccurrence, he could not rid himself of this suspicion. Stuck awake, he decided that he might as well pee.

Getting up, barely wanting to, Travis stumbled across the room. Just as he was about to enter the bathroom— Scratch, scratch.

Travis stopped and looked toward the other door that led out of the room. He did not remember the first sound but knew that was not the same sound.

Scratch, scratch.

His curiosity rose. The bathroom was not nearly as important as this. He wandered over, taking hold of the handle with a second of hesitation, then he opened the door. There was nothing there other than shadows.

He began to shut the door. Yap! came from downstairs. This time he did recognize the sound.

Nearly all of him just wanted to shut the door and lay back in bed. But that curiosity held like some strange addiction. Everything in his power told him to stay away, that there was nothing good to be found in the uncertainty, that only fear awaited those who sought it out. Yet, he had some strange desire to embrace the fear. That desire always won over rationality.

Travis first leaned out the door, looking around for anything. Nothing was there. He stepped out again, taking another second to check his surroundings. Nothing haunted. He took his time to slowly descend the steps. At the bottom of them, more caution followed more uneventfulness. He began to lose interest, beginning to listen to his conscience, about to return to the safety of his room.

Click, click, click, click, click, of nails ran across the wood floor. He turned his head toward the adjacent hallway. There was nothing. Click, click, click, click, click. Head snapped toward the kitchen. His eyes widened as he thought he might have seen something. But it was barely in his sight for a second and seemed no more than a shadow, close to the ground, racing across the entrance. But it could have been nothing more than a trick of the eyes.

Yap! Came from the room.

Definitely not his imagination. Those sounds were real. He was certain after hearing them this many times. He should just return to his room. Hell, he should leave the house completely. Yet, that felt irrational, if not completely irresponsible. This could not be a ghost or a burglar. It had to be an animal that somehow snuck into his place. He should get rid of it before it made a mess of his home.

Travis entered the kitchen with determined steps and flipped the light switch to rout out the nightly intruder. But none was found nor was there a trace of one. He wondered where whatever it was could have gone. For clarity's sake, he decided to check the sliding glass door, which was locked.

Standing before the pane, his reflection took over most of his view, but he could slightly see into the yard through his metaphysical self. There was an oddity that could only be described as a shadowy blob waiting outside. He immediately became worried that any sudden movements might cause it to run or, worse, charge. He remained still and stared. Nothing happened in those minutes that were continuing to stretch even now.

This stalemate could not keep going on. Travis flipped the porchlight on. Light illuminated the backyard and disintegrated the blob revealing a surprising lack of anything terrifying actually there. Instead, a mound of dirt was what he discovered. He was annoyed to have been spooked by a final f-you from the dog.

But before Travis was able to turn around and head back to bed, his attention was caught once more by dirt being flung out of the hole. This was where he should have walked away. But he had come too far for that. Especially now that fear had been replaced by irritation. The dog had been dealt with, but another animal had taken on the problematic role.

Travis threw open the door, which caused the digging to stop. He stormed out, hoping to catch the creature. However, standing over the hole, there was nothing within. Truly nothing within. It had been dug so deep that only a hollow abyss of unquestionable black filled the space. That seemed impossible at first. Then again, it must have been a mole or groundhog. The abyss beckoned a deeper examination to be certain. So, Travis leaned down to try seeing into the veil.

A low rumble could be heard. His first thought was something still digging even deeper. Then he realized the sound was a growl. Two glowing orbs appeared, eyes seeing prey. Travis drew back. At that same moment, a dog sprung out of the hole and bit his ankle. He screamed in pain. Then his scream became one of terror as he was pulled off his feet. The air was knocked out of him when he landed on his stomach. He gasped desperately. Fingers clawed the grass, ripping up clumps as he was dragged into the hole. The ground swallowed him hungrily.

Jordan and Oswald finally found their new home after being lost for so long in the fog.

Jordan, staring with his heterochromia eyes of sea-foam-green and golden-hazel, judged and approved, "The place looks nice."

"We did pick it out together," Oswald credited themselves.

Jordan reached over, cupping Oswald on the cheek before taking a finger and tracing over the scar on the bridge of his nose. "You found the place. I just liked it."

"And that's what matters," Oswald pampered.

Jordan smiled and then suggested, "Let's see the inside."

They parked in the driveway, walked the short path made of stone, and entered through the front door. Boxes of belongings and various furniture were placed around responsibly but with little consideration. Plenty of rearranging would be needed to add some fengshui. Regardless . . .

"Glad to see the movers had no trouble dropping our stuff off," Jordan commented.

"I'm going to check around," Oswald excused himself, going down a hallway, and then entered the kitchen. As he looked around the room, he could see through the sliding glass door. In the backyard was a dog, a beagle, digging a hole. He furrowed and rubbed his brow in frustration.

Jordan, peeking in through the doorway, saw the display. He asked as he entered the room, "What's going on?"

"There's a dog in our backyard," Oswald explained.

"Really?" Jordan was excitedly curious and came over to get a look. The pup made him smile. "Huh? I wonder whose dog that is?" Then he remembered the sour expression. "Are you upset about the digging?"

"Kind of," Oswald reluctantly admitted. It seemed a petty thing to be upset about.

"Well, we'll fill it in," Jordan assured. "So, stop pouting. You're going to age that cute face."

Oswald made no argument. He just wondered, "What should we do?"

"Let's go say hi," Jordan really wanted to.

"Okay," Oswald agreed, opening the door and offering the way.

They both stepped out into the back. The dog heard the door and turned his head to look, tail wagging. He turned around completely, running clumsily over, ears flopping. He sniffed and licked the offered hands and pant legs, circling around them, before taking a seat with a slight tilt to his hips and his head.

"Looks like he's smart," Jordan commented.

"Let's hope so," Oswald was not so sure. As a test, he asked, "Could you please stop digging?"

The dog made a whimper but seemed to respect the request as he turned around and began shoveling the dirt back into the hole.

"He is smart." Jordan was rather impressed.

Oswald was impressed too. So, he felt the need to ask, "Where's your master?"

The dog stopped for a moment, looked back again with a tilted head, then began digging the hole once again.

"You don't think . . ?" Jordan began.

". . . this dog belonged to the previous homeowner?" Oswald finished.

"And that they're . . ?"

"Buried on the property? I hope not."

Copper King Hotel

The suite suited the name of the establishment. Walls and carpet were the standard beige. The curtains, bed, nightstand, and dresser were lustrous beige. Perfect for the most boring royalty.

Oswald entered the room with a disappointed look, staring more toward the ground than actually looking around. He sighed. A complaint followed, "I can't believe we have to stay here tonight."

Jordan approached from behind, wrapping arms around Oswald, and a kiss was placed on his shoulder. Comfort was given to the situation, "I think this is fun. The place looks nice."

Jordan made his way further into the room to the bed where he plopped down on the end. One leg crossed over the other, and he lightly kicked as he leaned back on his arms. A playful smile on his face implied an interest.

Oswald raised his eyebrows in surprise. He reminded, "That seems kind of inappropriate right now. We did just find a dead body in our backyard."

"We already talked about that enough," Jordan dismissed. "And, apparently, I'll be examining the body tomorrow. I can give you all the gory details then, if you want. But right now, let's treat this like a little vacation before we settle into our home, and settle here in this city."

Oswald wanted to remain on this subject. However, he knew he thought too much. What he needed was to just be in the now. A beautiful man waited and wanted him. He forgot everything that did not matter at this moment so he could enjoy what was important.

The bags were dropped, the door was shut with a push, and Oswald made his way over. Jordan uncrossed his legs. Oswald sat on the lap of his lover. Arms wrapped around his waist. His hands rested on strong shoulders. They stared back at each other. Faces slowly drew closer until lips locked in a passionate kiss. Together, they fell back.

There was a soft rap on the door. The disturbance was delicate enough not to shake awake but, instead, kindly stir the occupants of the room. Oswald opened his eyes slowly. His first wonder was who could be there. Then he asked himself why they would even be knocking. He realized soon after that they had forgotten to put the 'Do Not Disturb' sign up.

The knock came again, not demanding to be answered, just acting as a reminder that someone was there. But the door needed to be answered before Jordan, still sleeping soundly, was awakened. Oswald slipped out stealthily from beneath his man, walked quietly across the room, and first checked the peephole before opening the door a crack.

In the hall waited a concierge that looked so old yet so young, looked so masculine yet so feminine, so ugly yet so beautiful.

Oswald spoke in a whisper, "How can I help you?"

"You have a guest waiting to see you," the soft speech was reciprocated.

"Who?" would even.

"A rather important member of Noir," the concierge informed.

"Why would one of them want to see me?" Oswald asked further.

"You'll be a professor at Eversound College," the concierge explained. "That'll make you an established member of our community."

Oswald paused to wonder how the concierge knew he would be working at the college. He came to the assumption that the guest must be another faculty member. If that was the case, it was best he went to make a proper impression. "Okay. Let me get dressed."

"No rush," said as a kindness.

Oswald shut the door, stepped back into the room, then took the time to look at Jordan, who still slept like a beauty in a fairytale. He should be left to rest. Oswald made a quick message on the provided notepad, 'Stepping out for a sec. Be back soon. Have my phone.' He dressed simply, gathered only the necessities, and exited.

"Ready," he exclaimed.

"Right this way."

Oswald was brought to a lounge setting. Leather upholstered booths offered both comfort and discretion. Low-blue lighting created an otherworldly sensation. And a bar took up one side of the room, filled with every expensive bottle one could procure.

The bartender casually wiped a glass. A few people sat here and there, talking in couples and small groups. Only one sat alone in the far corner. She looked like a prop that belonged in this ritzy establishment. Everyone here was wearing a fine suit or dress or, at least, their most formal clothes. But this woman seemed straight out of the Gothic era with her dark, frilled, over accentuated gown.

The concierge escorted Oswald over to her, speaking to the woman once reaching the table, "Good evening, Madam Rook. I brought—"

Madam Rook raised her hand to stop the introductions, though the way she gestured was not in a rude manner.

The concierge, smiling, gave a short bow and walked back from the table without another word.

Oswald stared at the woman for some time as he was left thinking. First, she seemed out of time. Second, she looked a lot like his mother. Third, she shared his last name.

"Please, call me Elise," she requested.

"Glad to meet you," Oswald greeted. "You wanted to see me?"

"How about you take a seat before we begin our conversation," Elise insisted.

"Of course." Oswald did as he was asked.

Elise stared at Oswald for a long time as if to take in his details, particularly that small scar on the bridge of his nose. She smiled. "You look healthy and handsome."

"Uh . . ." That comment was unexpectedly personal, causing both a blush and discomfort. "Thank . . . you? Who are you?"

"Your grandmother," answered honestly, then clarified, "five generations back from you."

Oswald was unbelieving. Such a claim would be impossible. If his great-great-grandmother was still alive, she would have to be over two hundred years old. This had to be a lie. Or maybe he was talking with a literal ghost. Or none of this was real at all.

"Your spirits," a waiter announced as he placed chilled champagne in a bucket of ice on the table along with two empty glasses and a glass of wine.

"Thank you," Elise said in appreciation. Then looked to Oswald. "Was there anything you wanted in particular? I ordered the champagne for us to share and celebrate. The wine's my one guilty pleasure."

"No," Oswald declined the offer.

Elise waved a hand to dismiss the attendant who left as graciously as the last.

Oswald followed up with a question, "What are we celebrating?"

Elise was prone to smiling a lot, it seemed. She gave one as she answered, "Getting this chance to meet you, of course. Now, would you do the honor of popping the cork?"

Oswald remained confused but, because of her happy disposition, he felt happy to oblige. He took the bottle, untwisted the wire seal, and popped the cork in a responsible manner. Elise clapped softly with joy. He smiled back, finding the situation enjoyable. A glass was poured for each, and they gave cheers.

"So," Elise began, taking on a semi-seriousness, "tell me, did you ever get to know Rosalyn?"

Oswald felt brought back to a curious state of mind. Rosalyn was his great-grandmother. Did Elise knowing that name validate her claim? Instead of putting too much thought into what was possible, he merely took a sip from his glass, let the alcohol relax away his suspicion, and spoke, "I only met her a few times. Whenever I would go over to my grandma's, she would take me to great-grandma's just down the road. I'll be honest, I barely remember a thing."

"I would love to hear about whatever you do remember," she seemed desperate to know.

"Well . . ." Oswald began to think. There really were not any memories, just feelings. "Her house smelled . . . old if that makes sense. And she and grandpa had these old wooden and plastic toys in a box that, every time I went over there, I would play with them."

"Thank you." She took time to delight in the simple description. Eventually, another want was brought up, "You mentioned your grandmother. I never got to meet Helaine. Or any of my grandchildren. Or great-grandchildren. But I'm blessed to meet you, Oswald."

"Would you like to know more about her?" Oswald offered. "About our family members?"

"I would very much like that." Elise smiled.

A knock on the door woke Jordan with a snort and a line of drool tracing down his cheek. He did not give much attention to his surroundings. Only the sound was on his mind as he tried to place it.

The knock came again. This time Jordan knew now that there was a visitor. He rolled out of bed, lazily lumbered across the room, and opened the door without caution.

Standing outside was a female concierge, young and not caring about anything, with braided black hair and pale skin.

"Hello?" Jordan hazily asked.

"You have a guest," she informed.

"Who?" The question needed to be asked as always.

"Your father."

That was weird. Jordan scowled as if hearing a sick joke. His response came out stricken, "My dad's dead."

"I'm well aware," that was not a surprise for her to hear. "He's still here to see you."

Jordan became confused by her assurance. He looked to the bed to discover Oswald was not there or anywhere in the room for that matter. The sudden disappearance of him without a word was out of character. Then there was this girl who appeared like a caricature. Nobody looked like this normally, especially when working in a fine establishment. Something was certainly wrong. Jordan decided to go along to discover what.

"Let me get dressed," Jordan stated.

"I'll be waiting."

The dining room was large, able to host important venues, though there were very few people currently dining this late. Dozens of unoccupied, cloth-draped tables filled the space. A large crystal chandelier provided a heavenly orange light that contrasted with the blackness of the ten o'clock night.

Jordan looked around the room skeptically, searching for the promised ghost. His eyes grew wide in disbelief. Sitting at one of the tables was a middle-aged black man, hair curly and having started to recede. That was his dad.

Mr. Setly noticed that he had been noticed and gave a smile and wave.

All of Jordan's reactions happened near simultaneously. Tears burst from his eyes. He covered the bottom half of his face to hold back an outcry. His body curled forward to try forcing it, which made him fall to his knees. Behind his hand, he sobbed.

Mr. Setly was flabbergasted. He quickly got up from his chair, rushed over, and kneeled in front of his son.

"You're not supposed to be here," Jordan said in denial.

"But I am here," Mr. Setly assured.

"How?" Jordan wanted an answer.

Mr. Setly became withdrawn, uncertain if he could or should explain. The thing was, "It doesn't matter. I'm here now. Let's spend what time we have together." He placed a hand on his son's shoulder for comfort.

Jordan, not able to vocally agree without blubbering, nodded.

"Alright." Mr. Setly stood up, taking hold of Jordan by the arm to help him onto his feet. "Let's eat."

They made their way over to the table, sitting across from each other. Mr. Setly took up his menu and began looking it over. Though Jordan had taken hold of his, he was distracted, looking at his dad intently with those powerful heterochromia eyes of sea-foam-green and golden-hazel.

Mr. Setly became aware of the stare, taking the time to set down his menu, and speak, "How have you been? How many years has it even been?"

"Nine years," Jordan answered the latter.

"Nine years!?" the announcement was loud with surprise. "It's been a really long time since that day—"

"The day you died," Jordan specified.

"Yeah," Mr. Setly sadly acknowledged. A long pause followed before something needed to be made right, "I'm sorry."

"Why are you apologizing?" Jordan shook his head disapprovingly. "You couldn't have known what was going to happen."

"I know," Mr. Setly admitted. "But you still deserve an apology. I left you. Whether or not that was my choice, I left you."

"Stop," Jordan choked. "You did nothing wrong."

"Is that true?" The feeling was confronted.

Jordan looked away in shame. He sighed, knowing, "Yes, you did nothing wrong. But . . ." There was pain that had been felt and blame that had been placed, "I've started to hate you."

Mr. Setly was saddened but understood. "You have every right to hate me."

"There's so much that you missed out on," Jordan declared. "There is so much I never had the chance to get closure for. All these unanswered questions have always haunted me."

"Well," Mr. Setly assured, "you can tell me now."

"I don't know if I can," Jordan put up a wall. "There is so much distance between us now, literally life and death."

"Then don't," that was okay too because, "I love you, Jordan."

"But would you always love me?" Jordan remained uncertain.

"Of course," the promise was made.

"Even if I was gay?" The fact was put out there.

Mr. Setly was taken aback for a moment. He had genuinely not expected his son to be that. It was not something he hated nor something he knew how to deal with. But, after just a moment's thought, he settled into quick acceptance because, "I love you, Jordan. No matter who you are."

"Well, I'm gay," Jordan unsurprisingly revealed.

"What a shock," Mr. Setly joked. "And I'm proud of you."

Jordan felt himself relieved of an immense weight. So many years of repressed sexuality combined with what was thought to be endless uncertainty if his dad could have accepted him was now gone. Holy shit. There was no way this was real. Being given this chance had to be nothing more than a dream. Still, dream or not, he found himself becoming unburdened. Needing that extra assurance, he asked, "Are you really okay with that?"

59

"Why wouldn't I be?" The question earnestly questioning the question. The answer was obvious, "Your sexuality doesn't change who you are. And you are my son, who I love."

Jordan started crying again, wiping one tear away at a time.

"It's okay," Mr. Setly comforted.

"I know." Jordan was calming down; tears mostly faded at this point, leaving his cheeks red from the constant rubbing. "I just never believed I would get to tell you. And I never knew if you could accept me."

"I'll say it again. I love you, Jordan. I'll accept you always."

"I love you, dad." Jordan truly did feel the meaning behind those words.

"So," now began the snooping, "do you have anybody?"

"I do," pridefully admitted. "His name's Oswald. He just got his master's degree and will be teaching at the college in this city. He's an amazing man."

"Sounds like one," Mr. Setly agreed. "What about you? Did you end up going to college to become a doctor?"

"I did go to medical school . . ." Jordan became more embarrassed by this question than the previous one, "But . . . I didn't become a doctor. Turns out I don't deal with living people that well. Instead, I became a coroner."

"You're the most social person I know," Mr. Setly refuted.

"I like people," there was no denying that, "but I don't have the patience to deal with patients."

"Well," shrugging, "working with the dead—" Mr. Setly stopped himself as he watched the waitress approach.

"I'm sorry to interrupt," she offered her condolences. "Is there anything I can start you off with?"

"Oh," Jordan had completely forgotten they were getting dinner. "We've been so busy talking that neither of us has really gotten a chance to look at the menu. I'm sorry."

"It's completely fine," she assured. "I can come back."

"Actually," Mr. Setly interjected, "I think we're ready to order. I'll have the prime rib, medium rare, with a side of mash potatoes and buttered broccolini."

"Wonderful choice." She turned to Jordan. "And for you?"

Jordan quickly shoved his face into the menu to try and make a sudden decision. Everything looked so good. But the real question was, 'what was he in the mood for?'

"He'll get your burger," Mr. Setly ordered for Jordan.

"What temp?" She was about to go through the various decisions one had to make when ordering a burger.

"A little pink is fine, all the toppings, and a side of fries," Mr. Setly answered them all before they were asked.

"Wonderful. I'll have that put in for you right away."

"Actually," Jordan had some input. "Veggie burger."

"Can do." And she was gone.

Mr. Setly looked at his son and smiled. "You've always been so indecisive and would look at the menu for over an hour and still not know what you'd want. But I know you'd want a burger. No matter where your mother and I took you as a kid, you ordered one. Even

Chinese restaurants if they had them. Though the veggie burger is different."

Jordan blushed at how spot on his father was for the most part. "You do know me."

"So, tell me about everything that's been going on in your life."

Oswald tilted his glass all the way back to finish off his champagne. He smiled widely, shutting his eyes, and took a breath. The alcohol was making him tired, adding to the effects of the late night.

"It has been good," Elise commented.

"It has," Oswald could not help but agree.

"Even so, I think we should bring this to an end," the time was approaching one in the morning.

"You're probably right." He sighed.

"I'm glad we had this chance to meet." She smiled.

He smiled back. "Me too—"

Oswald wobbled sideways. His arm reached out, catching himself against a wall. He looked around, discovering he was in a hallway. How he got here was a mystery. Everything was hazy in his head, fading in and out of blackness. He definitely drank too much.

Body pushed forward to open a door, and he fell through the entryway. Balance was regained while standing and swaying in the middle of the hotel room. Looking toward the bed saw Jordan asleep. Oswald smiled, stripped down, and snuck back under the covers.

Jordan, half a burger left on his plate, yawned. It was only eleven-thirty but being stuffed made him lazy with a wanting to lie down.

"You always had a small appetite," Mr. Setly remarked happily.

"I know." Jordan yawned again.

"Seems like you're ready to go to bed," the yawn a clear sign.

"I wish I wasn't," Jordan said in disappointment. "I wish this could go on for longer."

"I do too," Mr. Setly shared the sentiment. "But I think we've said the important things. You should take care of yourself."

"You're right." Another yawn followed. "It's time to say goodbye." Jordan felt his face scrunch in pain. Brow furrowed. Lips squeezed together and quivered. A slow blink tried to equalize the building feelings. But the moment they reopened, he exhaled a sharp breath and heaved forward slightly. Teeth chattered. Then tears began to flow.

Oswald was slipping on a sock as he took in a breath to energize his body.

Jordan rolled in the sheets, stretching, moaning, and then stared softly at Oswald.

"Good morning," Oswald gave a greeting.

Jordan lifted his head, let it drop back on the pillow, covered his face for a moment to wipe away the sleep, then proclaimed, "I had such a strange dream."

"Really?" Oswald shared the sentiment. When he woke, he first thought that the meeting with his great-great-grandmother was real. But, based on how much he supposedly drank, he should have woken up hungover.

Feeling perfectly fine made him question the whole experience. "What was your dream about?"

Jordan thought back to try putting the pieces together. Happiness and sadness melded into a conflicting feeling that wetted eyes and turned up lips. "It was about my dad."

"That's amazing." Oswald knew the difficulties of Jordan's past. "What happened exactly?"

"We just talked and had dinner." That was enough.

"Sounds amazing," Oswald felt.

But the fantasy could not be enjoyed forever as Jordan knew, "Time for work."

Elise stood in front of the auditorium, waiting patiently with fifty or so others. Beside her was a middle-aged black man. Almost every part of her wanted to keep to herself because of shyness. But she was in a great mood after being given the chance to talk with Oswald. She let her guard and introversion down to turn toward the man.

"How was your visit?" Elise asked.

Mr. Setly looked at her, glancing around first to make certain she was referring to him before responding kindly, "It went great."

"Who did you get to see?" She was truly curious.

"My son," Mr. Setly said happily. "You?"

"My great-great-grandson," she shared the glee. After a pause, pursing her lips in a scrunched smile as she thought, her selfishness was also shared, "This was more about me wanting to connect with a family I lost when my daughter left the town. We never talked after that. I never got to see her kids. My only regret was putting this town above my own family. This chance has let me know where my priorities belong."

"I think all of us here are selfish," Mr. Setly professed. "I came to help my son find the closure he needed. But, as his father, that's what I wanted."

"Would you call that selfish selflessness?"

"That's exactly what that is."

Their conversation came to an end at the sound of high-heeled feet clicking loudly on the stage.

A professional woman walked up to a microphone and addressed everybody in the room, "I am so glad to have you visit from the other side. Here at Copper King, our goal has always been to reconnect the living with the dead. Life can be hard for both when there is unfinished business. I hope that you and your loved ones have been able to resolve what was left behind . . ."

Guardian of Knowledge

Knowledge is power, meaning there is no force more powerful than academia, for that is where minds come together, information is stored, and subjects are taught.

Oswald arrived at Eversound College much earlier than needed. His first lecture would not start until eleven. And the faculty meeting, intended to welcome him, would not be starting until ten. That gave him an hour to himself.

Already knowing the layout well enough to know where he needed to go for when he needed to be there, there was little interest in exploring. His real want was to see the library. He heard that the collection consisted of a million items, some of rare antiquity. The pictures online were persuading but, now standing outside the building, he was convinced that the collection existed.

He pushed through the heavy wooden doors, then through another set, only to find him barred by a turnstile. Seeing them reminded him of the days when one could freely go in and out of a library. But modern times were here. He could not be upset by the necessary security.

Unfortunately, this was an inconvenience. To get through required something to be scanned, that thing of which he did not have. His only choice was to talk to the attendant in the room.

"Excuse me," Oswald got attention from the girl sitting behind the desk, "How do I get in?"

She eyed him curiously as if the question already excluded him from entering. "Are you new here?"

"Very new," he answered. "Today's my first day."

"Well, you just need to swipe your student ID." She acted out the gesture.

"Not a student."

"Oh," an exclaim of surprise. To her, he seemed too young to be a professor. Still, she explained, "Well, teachers are issued badges by the administration."

"I don't have one," he admitted. "I guess they'll be giving me that during the faculty meeting. But I arrived an hour early in hopes I could see the library first. Is there any way you can let me in? I completely understand if not. I'll just come back later."

"Well . . ." she used that word again as she thought of what to do. He was being so kind and understanding. He seemed like he could be trusted. Of course, there was no just letting anybody in. What she needed was, "Can I see your ID? A driver's license or state-issued will be fine. I'll check the registry."

He smiled as he took out his rainbow wallet, pulled out his ID, and handed it over.

She looked at the picture, comparing the image with the person. They matched, the scar on the bridge of his nose a clear identifier. Then she saw the name. "Oswald Rook? You know this school was founded by the Rook family. Happen to be a relative?"

Oswald shrugged. "Maybe. I don't really know anything about my ancestry. Wouldn't it be crazy if I actually was?"

"Crazy?" That was not the word. "Amazing, I'd say. That would mean this whole place belongs to you."

He considered the fortune of that for a moment and, "I couldn't agree more. But it is crazy. And what's even crazier is that last night I had a dream I was drinking with my great-grandmother, Elise."

"Elise?" Another surprising exclamation. "Elise Rook was the founder of this city and the founder of this school. Are you trying to trick me?" Tone playful.

"Not at all." He waved his hands back and forth to erase the thought. "It was just a dream. I'm pretty sure

I heard her name somewhere and associated myself with her because, you know, we have the same last name."

"Well . . ." handing the ID back, she quickly typed away on the computer and discovered, "You are in the system. You teach anthropology?"

"I do," he said proudly. "With a focus on religion and mythology."

"You'll fit right in Darkess," she remarked. "And I think you'll be happy with our selection. We have a lot of bizarre, occulty books. Just go down the stairs in the middle of the room and, from where you step off, go to the very far back, left corner."

"Down?" He asked since this was the ground floor.

"We have a few lower levels."

"How many?" He could not help questioning.

Instead of an answer, she directed, "I'm going to push a button. You go through when I do."

He nodded to acknowledge he understood.

Down the first flight but no more. Oswald was curious to see how many levels there were, just not today. He only had a limited time and did not want to get lost, which would have been easy. Not only were there lower floors but there were also higher ones. By going too far down, he might forget how many he would need to go back up.

In the corner, he found what he hoped for, sort of. The books consisted almost entirely of horoscopes, modern-day Wicca, and basic folklore. Most of this stuff was surface layer information that entertained children and childish adults. Honestly, it seemed impossible this was all the school had, and in such a limited space. He took a quick look around but did not find any other

68

related sections. The only explanation he could think of was that any other material was on a lower floor. So, he decided . . .

One floor lower, he checked the same location and found another occult section. These were of relatively the same quality as those above, though having a bit more serious tone. The small change made him wonder.

On a whim, he went down again to find books that were even better. His suspicions seemed to be true, that the complexity of the books was based on the floor. That meant the lowest level would have what he really wanted to see.

He never went all the way to the lowest possible floor. Three more flights down, which was six in total, was where he stopped. That was because it seemed as if down was an infinite spiral toward the center of the world, beyond the world, in fact, reaching into a chasm of other worlds. He did not have the time to debunk the thought, nor did he want to risk getting lost.

As before, he checked the back corner. Elation. He had found works that were more to what he expected. And if these were here, and there were many more floors below, what more could there be? He was excitedly curious to know. But that would have to be saved for another day. Right now, he would indulge in what he had.

Ta, ta, ta.

Oswald casually turned his head toward where he heard the pitter-patter. There was nothing along the aisle or at the end.

Ta, ta, ta.

He turned fully this time to face the bookshelf behind him. He had not been remotely concerned when first hearing the noise. What he saw changed that, leaving him paralyzed. Through the shelving, eyes stared directly at him. They were big and vicious as they determined their prey.

Whatever was there turned away to vanish from sight. Ta, ta, ta. The sound let him know that the thing was not gone but going around the shelf.

Oswald could tell which direction and began moving the other way. His instincts told him to run, but his rationality convinced him otherwise. He did not pretend that this experience was in his head but, instead, there had to be an explanation. Or perhaps he was making a bigger deal than this had to be. Regardless, what he saw spoke volumes, demanding him to leave, and he obliged, making his way back to the stairs.

Ta. Ta. Ta. Followed right behind at a slow pace. Those killer eyes could be felt watching.

Oswald could not make a misstep or else . . . who knows? He did not want to find out. So, every step was careful as he made his way to the stairs. And as he reached them, he reached out his hand to grab the railing. That was when he realized he still held one of the books. It should not have been an issue, and yet because of his recollection, the thing behind him seemed to notice as well. There came a higher-pitched growl.

He slowly lowered down to set the book on the floor. But that did not matter in the least. His accident was already taken as attempted theft. Murderous intent was strong. The steps began approaching.

There were no more excuses in his mind. Maybe he was thinking irrationally. But being alive and acting ridiculous was better than keeping his cool only to die. Instincts screamed run and he did.

Heavy 'tunts' chased. The entire stairwell was vibrated by each bound that was closer than the last. The tambour of the growl became deeper like that of a hungry death rattle.

Oswald could almost feel claws reaching toward him. He could not help imagining the pain of being caught by a single swipe. How his flesh would tear. That pushed him to move faster.

Relief rose as he was almost to the ground floor. Or was he? Time suddenly froze as the thought caught him in a moment of fear. How many flights had he gone up? He had not been counting. He knew he needed to go up six, but did he already go up two or three? If he was wrong, he might be dead.

Then the distress was paused as Oswald neared the next floor, slowing his next few steps before stopping because the Dean, Milton Maypot, stood on the plateau. A quick glance back was made, but there was nothing. Then attention returned forward, and he greeted with a breathy heave, "Hello, Dean."

"Oswald Rook, I presume?" Dean Maypot spoke. "I hope our library is to your liking."

"Unsettling," was Oswald's honest, immediate answer. "I felt like I was being chased just now. But that's probably me being paranoid."

"No, you're not . . ." A black, hairless cat hopped up the steps, passed Oswald, and began intertwining between Dean Maypot's legs. "This is Bastet. She protects the books."

"I was scared of a cat," Oswald gave an airy chuckle. "Felt like I was being chased by a lion." Also, "Bastet, you say? Named after the Egyptian Goddess?"

"It seems you do know your stuff," Dean Maypot praised. "I'm glad we hired you before others saw your potential." Bastet perked and ran off. "There she goes. We should be off ourselves. The faculty meeting will begin shortly."

In the depths of the library, the shadows grew thicker and thicker the deeper down, eating the light from everywhere, from the fixtures, and from torchlights. This was good for the man. At least he believed so. Darkness tended to benefit thieves.

He skulked a hundred floors down, though there were hundreds more he could have descended to. On each lower level, he would have found even grander and more omnipotent books and works filled with true magic, from Otherworlds and planes of existence, written by the very Gods. But they were not what he sought. More accurate to say they were not what he had been hired to steal.

His contractor was not interested in Otherworlds but in this world and its creations and its meaning, the knowledge known as 'Dreamtime.' However, though there were many stories told by ancient peoples, time had distorted the lore, losing the truth and the power once known. The fragmented information could never be compiled into something accurate. What was needed was a recorded text from that time long ago.

Only one place had ever existed that held such knowledge. But the Library of Alexandria burned down more than two thousand years ago. Then again, a place filled with materials from lands across the world, from times long ago, that held magic that was now forgotten, could have easily relocated. Who was to say that the burning was not staged to protect this vault?

The contractor discovered the truth. Now, though the thief knew nothing other than a paycheck, he found himself searching the labyrinth. Many days and nights were spent sneaking to avoid the staff and whatever else may be lurking. And the hundredth floor was where he discovered a fabled tome that he had been sent to get. It was stuffed into his satchel, and he could finally leave.

The attack was swift and silent. From above, the beast had sprung. Paws pushed the thief to the floor, and fangs buried into his throat. A sharp jerk snapped his neck, killing with little blood.

Standing on two feet that had become humanlike, and reaching with a hand reshaped from a paw, the tome was retrieved and placed back on the rightful spot.

From the end of the aisle appeared Dean Maypot. "Allow me to apologize for Mr. Rook's intrusion."

"I was not worried about him," Bastet remarked in the noble tone of a Goddess. "I could sense that he did not seek power. No. What he craves is knowledge. He is the type of person I welcome to my library."

"But aren't power and knowledge one and the same?" Dean Maypot posed.

Bastet smiled at the notion. "They very much are the same. As are pride and confidence. And stubbornness and determination. But what makes them different?"

"Motivation," Dean Maypot answered without having to think. "Whether they are selfish or selfless."

"And what motivated you to hire Mr. Rook?" She challenged.

He smiled just as she had. "I am a selfish man."

"As you are," she agreed. "But still a man I trust."

"And I thank you. Now then," changing the subject, "what to do with the body?"

"Leave it to be fed on."

Oswald could not wait until the end of the day. He returned to the library during one of his extended breaks between classes. A part of him wanted to get some books that he had forgotten to check out during his unnecessary panic. He also wanted reassurance that

73

there was no need for him to have panicked the way he did.

There was no anxiety whatsoever as he stood at the stairwell. Instead, confusion and a little disappointment were felt. No longer did the descent appear infinite. The bottom floor was very clearly visible.

Furthermore, when he went down, he discovered there were only five lower levels. But he was certain he had gone down six the first time. His doubt was only reinforced when checking the shelves to not find any of the books he had seen before. His thought, regardless of how ridiculous, was that there must be secret levels.

A 'meow,' broke his crazy consideration. Casually he turned his head toward where he heard the call. There was Bastet, the cat, at the end of the aisle.

She eyed him before turning to wander away, stopping for a moment to look back as if urging him to follow, then continued.

He did follow to another corner of the room. There he found a second section of books, the books he had seen when he was on what he thought to be the sixth level. He guessed it must have been his imagination. To think he was actually beginning to believe in hidden floors. How silly. He must have just been tired.

Bleeding Heart Romantic

Two stood at a bus stop on a muggy evening. One was a hauntingly beautiful girl. The other was a phantom-like adolescent boy. They did not know each other, merely strangers waiting for the same reason, though their destinations may vary.

Him, Isiah, was a quiet sort. Little did he speak but much did he think. Those thoughts were always written down in a notebook that was always on his person, everything important was then recorded on his computer at home. And today, at this very moment, he was struck by inspiration.

The scribbling of a pen on paper caught the girl's attention. She could not help but ask, "What's that you're writing?"

Isiah was caught by surprise at her inquiry, having not even noticed her standing right beside him. Not a surprise, of course. He hardly ever paid attention to people. Now that he was dragged into a conversation, he looked and noticed she was around his age and extremely beautiful. He responded in his awkward way, "Would you like to see?" When, in actuality, he did not want to share.

The girl chuckled. "That would be impossible," she remarked as she turned her head to reveal why. Her eyes were cloudy, silver marbles. She was blind.

"Oh, I'm sorry," he felt the need to offer condolence. "It was just a turn of phrase. I didn't mean to be rude."

"I guess you owe me," she responded in a joking demand. "How about you read me whatever it is you're writing?"

"What if it's something embarrassing or boring?" he struggled to accept her terms.

"You were so willing to show me," she challenged.

"Well . . ." knowing he did not even want to show, "yeah . . . that's a lot less embarrassing than reading it out loud."

"Fine," she dismissed with an arrogant disregard. Just a ploy. An effective ploy.

Isiah felt guilted into giving what she wanted. Starting by looking at his recent scribblings and reading several times over to review before sharing, he soon began . . .

"My Sweet Lady Death,
How you take my breath.

"Beautiful beyond compare.
One like you is so rare.
Let me show I care
By giving thee my air.

"I gladly give my life,
One of strife,
For you to be my wife.
A vow sealed by a cut of this knife.

"But should I dare
Presume we can be a pair?
My feelings, are you aware?
Assuming so is unfair.

"Though, surrounded by lies,
I'd rather be swarmed by flies.
I've already said my goodbyes.
Happily, I'll plunge to my demise.

"At my wrist, I stare,
Inflicting a simple tear.
I cannot help but glare,
At the moment of pain, I bear.

"The blood is a lot,
And to you, I am brought,
Entering your embrace which I sought.
Now, together, let us rot.

"How you take my breath,
My Sweet Lady Death."

Isiah lowered the paper, satisfied overall, though still unhappy and uncertain.

The girl chuckled.

He glanced her way reflexively. For that short time, he had forgotten she was there. Her laughter, as a cruel cue, reminded him and he felt hurt. But this was the expected response. Poetry was uncool.

"I'm sorry," she sensed his distress and was quick to make an apology. "I wasn't laughing because I thought it was bad. I really did like it. I just find it ironic. Is that a love confession or a suicide note?"

He pondered on what the intended meaning of his work was and knew right away, "Can't it be both?"

"Are you saying you're in love with Death?" Asked as a whimsical interest.

"Death's always on my mind," he admitted, "A sign of infatuation. So, I guess I am."

"Is it the idea of Death or Death personified?" She delved with now keen curiosity.

Confusion struck as he realized that they were having a real conversation. That was not something he was used to. Though, that came to an end right then and there as the bus pulled up. With the chance to run away presented, he got on. But getting away was not so easy since, after taking his seat, the girl sat beside him.

"Why didn't you answer my question?" she playfully remarked as if insulted.

"Sorry," he gave immediately. But if she was looking for a genuine response, he had none. Instead, he turned to stare out the window to avoid eye contact which, thinking about it, made no sense. She was blind. Still. . .

She pressed, "Just not going to talk to me? I know it's you I sat by."

He thought of how to answer, and what he thought made him feel embarrassed, blushing and continuing to avoid facing her as well as avoid speaking.

Sensing his feelings, she remarked, "You don't have to say if you're shy."

"I'm not shy," he was quick to lie to try showing some bravado for this cute girl.

Again, reading him, she sarcastically berated, "Of course not. You're a tough guy. What a shame. Personally, I like sensitive souls."

"Doesn't every woman say that?" He retorted with the use of the rude, cliché line.

"Most do," she admitted with a slight rise in her tone as if ready to be insulted by his insinuation. "And most actually do want that. But," clearly on the attack now, "the guy that assumes he is sensitive or assumes he is nice often doesn't realize how wrong he is about himself."

. . . "I never said I was nice," Isiah declared. "So, leave me alone."

The girl sat for a moment longer in thought. "You're definitely not a 'nice guy,'" she said with sarcasm as she exhaled through her nose as a laugh. "You're not entitled. You're not pushy. You're not arrogant. What I see is someone kind. Someone gentle. Someone compassionate. Someone vulnerable. You are also in pain. I can tell that much from your poetry."

Isiah had no response to her analysis.

Sigh. "I thought us meeting the way we did might have been fate," was her hope. Disappointingly, "I guess that was just wishful thinking." She waited just a little longer, wanting to be stopped, but was not as she got up and changed seats.

Isiah continued to stare out the window now that he was left alone to reflect on his behavior. He knew right away that he had been in the wrong. His comment, though not intended to be, was sexist even though all he was doing was doubting any BS. His problem was not with her, or women, but with people in general. But really his problem was himself because he did not understand people. He could not trust them, and everything they said always sounded like a lie. Paranoia left him isolated. He accepted that because, in the end, his inability to trust had him ruin everything as he had just done and would do again.

Even so . . . After Isiah pulled the cord that brought the bus to a stop, and he began to make his way to the door, there was a pause as he stood beside the seat where the girl had moved to. She paid him no mind, not aware of who was even getting off or on. But his one word, "Sorry," did not seem to catch her by surprise. Her head tilted only slightly, and she smiled just as barely. He continued down the aisle and exited.

On the street, he looked back to the bus for no reason that he could explain. To his wonder, eyebrows raising, the girl was looking out, as if staring directly at him. He turned away and began toward home as they traveled their separate ways.

79

The east side of Darkess was a particular place of neglect. The streets were paved, but the discarded paper remnants of litter could be found jammed into corners and crevasses, clogging drainage grates. The grass was green, but overgrowth made the sidewalks overrun by shrubbery and branches, while the disregard for where to walk made the ground patchy. Houses had a unique and attractive architecture, but properties were left in a state of decay, discolored by mold. This degrading was caused by those very people who complained about the dirtiness of the neighborhood.

Isiah stood outside the house where he lived, which was never his home. This pause was always taken each time he returned. He needed to ponder whether he should enter or turn away and never come back. The latter was not an option. That was what he had convinced himself anyway. As a boy still in high school without a job or any work experience, there was no way he could take care of himself. And, even if he succeeded in gaining some kind of financial freedom, he knew nothing about the skills of independence; How to pay bills. Taxes. Insurance. He did not even know how to drive. Of course, when push came to shove, he always learned quickly, adapted when needed, and survived. But he would rather avoid doing any of that if there was another option. So, he would always enter this place that never cared about him.

What greeted him inside was the unpleasant smell of left-out dishes, piled-up clothes, and dirty carpeting. Nobody took care of this place except for him, a responsibility which he gave up on hoping that others would try keeping things clean as they got worse. But nobody seemed to notice even after nearly two weeks. And, honestly, he no longer gave a damn either.

This place was only a rest at night. Leaving as soon as he awoke was the routine, as was making a beeline back to his bedroom when he returned. Eyes were almost always held to the ground as he passed through. Only the archway in the hall drew his gaze into the room. Sometimes there was nothing. That was most of the time, in fact. But there were those days.

Passed out on the couch were the blue collared junkie and his girlfriend. Both were victims of the opioid epidemic, driven into the embrace of the narcotic dream that freed them from the monsters of reality. But the man, in particular, was a victim of his own pride. He could not admit he put his faith in the wrong people who only took advantage of his arrogance and ignorance. Time and time again, he would instead blame anybody that did not agree with his ideals, even if they were trying to help. He was a terrible father figure that never gave guidance.

Isiah looked away, now numb to the sight he had seen hundreds of times before. There was nothing he could do. Not like he had not tried before. But those attempts were painful and in vain. As long as he minded his own business, his space was not intruded on. At least that was how it had been.

Entering his room, he placed his bag on the ground and tossed his notebook on his desk, landing with a smack. He was momentarily stunned. Something was missing.

All around was blackness that was not darkness. Isiah looked at his hands and could see they were completely visible, not veiled by any shadows. An abnormality, but not one that was concerning, at least not to him. He was rather calm about the situation. He had spent most of his life in nothingness, dreaming of nothingness, believing in nothingness, remembering nothingness. This might as well have been any other day or night, which this could be for all he knew. Experiencing the world from the cage of his mind was something very much like this. His only recourse was to walk through, regardless that he might be going nowhere.

Footsteps sounded like water droplets, each creating an outward pulse on the non-existent floor and rippling into the endlessness. The sound resonated with Isiah like a tuning fork meant to balance his chaotic mind. The sensation was both disturbing and calming. Goosebumps rushed over his skin.

Slowly a scene faded in. There was a bench made of wood and cast iron, not comfortable but convenient. A post, shaped to point toward a direction, reading 'Styx.' And a girl, blind eyes familiar, beckoning.

Isiah seated himself beside her.

A long silence lingered. Then she spoke, "Is this how you envisioned your stories would end?" Her question shattered the stillness.

"I always knew this was how things would end," Isiah admitted. "In those moments of clarity, I could recognize that one day I would be consumed by my madness. I couldn't say for sure when, but there was no doubt that eventually, I was going to kill myself. Though, a part of me did believe I would have at least been in my forties. But tragedy strikes without remorse."

"I can't help but agree with you there. However, did you really think that acknowledging and accepting your own suicide was during a moment of clarity?"

A long hush occurred to challenge the notion. Isiah thought deeply about how he felt when the monster began to take control, when he was the monster, and who he was when the monster was gone. Manic. Depressant. Calm.

She broke the empty pause again with her continuing dialog, "I'm certain that in those truly clear moments, suicide never even crossed your mind. Not when. Not how. You just lived without those considerations."

Calm, huh? Isiah questioned. In that calmness following the storm of his emotions, was he really clear-minded? There was no way that would be possible. A survivor of a wreck is not okay immediately afterward. More so, she was right. Before these terrible feelings and the time long passed, the thought to end his life did not exist. They were only there at the beginning, while during, and the after. So, was that place he thought to be clear really just another fog? "I think you might be right."

"Only you can be the one to decide that."

"Aren't I already doing that?" He analyzed the situation to its most logical conclusion as he often did when his emotions were handled and packed away. "Isn't this just my mind interpreting my final moments as I die? Everything you said is just my subconscious coming to terms with my actions? Why else would it be you in this void, the last person I had an honest interaction with?"

"You can believe what you want," she left the situation vague.

With the lack of clarification, Isiah took to looking up and off in the distance as he seemed to drift away.

"You're just going to leave me here alone?" Said with a tilted head and gaze that shifted away.

"I guess," he said flatly, not guilted by her expression in the least. "All that's really left to do is fade."

"Seems rude even if this is your own disillusion," she teased. "You should give a girl all your attention even in the afterlife. Or at least try taking advantage of the situation."

"I was never that kind of guy," he admitted.

"Well, I'm that kind of girl. So, rest your head on my lap," and she reached out to take his shoulders, slowly pulling him to lay him down, which he allowed. "The bus doesn't arrive for a few more minutes. I want to talk a little longer while we have the chance. Treat this as your mind still needing to resolve other issues if you must."

"Are you real?" he questioned instead.

"Why ask that now?" the idea was played around with.

"Because I never would have imagined this even among my deepest fantasies," he believed to be true.

"You really aren't that kind of guy," she repeated his words back to him. "That's probably why you were so lonely. You held everybody at a distance because you could never trust any of them. But you were also so selfless that you never put pressure on a single person to be involved in your life. If anything, you pushed them away because you didn't want others to feel used by you. Yet, even after all of that, you continued to live. So, what suddenly changed?"

"My dad's girlfriend stole my laptop and sold it to fuel their drug addiction," Isiah recalled. "And my dad didn't care. Apparently, everything I owned I owed to him because of how much effort he had been putting into raising me. As if he actually did anything. Not to mention that I paid for the computer with my own money."

"Seems rather extreme to end your life over a possession," she stated with bold criticism but did not hold judgment.

"I couldn't care less about the device," he clarified. "What was important was everything that I had saved to it. All of my writings."

"Doesn't that sound far more ridiculous? Why were you so grief-stricken at the loss of a few words?"

"It is stupid." He was well aware. But it still made all the sense in the world, especially during those times he lost his mind. "I have no friends. No family. I only had those words. They were mine. They were my world. They were me. Everything I was. Everything I went through. The years and years of work. My pain expressed. All gone like they never mattered."

"What if they didn't matter?" The question was put out there and left hanging to approach the situation slowly. "Maybe you want them to matter, so you have an excuse not to change because, without them, the person you created can't truly exist anymore. Now, you have been left to redefine yourself. It can be miserable having to start over, terrifying even. That's why most don't. They just give up. Are you going to give up?—"

The bus arrived before an answer.

"It's your time to get on," she ordered and gave him two coins.

"Across the River Styx?" Isiah said jokingly.

"You already crossed even if you don't remember," she told. "But I'm sending you back over."

"Why?"

"I really liked the poem you wrote me," she admitted.

"Are you my Lady Death?"

"My name is Tia. Now, go."

Isiah was the first and last on the bus as no other would be so lucky to leave the afterlife. The driver, made of bone and shadows, waited patiently for him to take his seat near the back. Then the machine drove on, drifting silently like a rolling fog.

The road was treacherous, crossing over a bog of tar, through a field of brittle bones, and then along a sheer cliff on a narrow pass. Everything threatened to drag them down. Yet the driver never seemed to waiver with concern, having become accustomed to the route

85

after centuries. Isiah did not worry either, knowing he was already dead, so dying again made no difference.

They came to a tunnel at the peak, one of industrial construction. The circular passage was carved straight through the craggy mountain. Dull, orange lights lit the way, their spacing creating a strobe effect while passing beneath. Once through, the bus found itself on a familiar road, one that many used to come and go from Darkess.

Heading toward downtown, the bus came to its first stop, opening doors to allow a spirit on. Stop after stop picked up more spirits and shades as they made their way around the city. By the end, with nearly every seat filled, they reached St. Kindred Hospital. This was the place to get off.

Isiah entered the building, walked past the front desk, and made his way through the halls with the foreknowledge of exactly where he was headed. Nobody bothered him since nobody could see him because he was a spirit.

He found his hospital room and himself hooked up to monitors. But he also found someone he never expected. His mother rested in a chair by his bedside.

Eyes opened to discover that her son had awoken from his vegetative state.

"What are you doing here?" Isiah asked.

"I needed to be here after hearing what happened," she answered with an edge that became anger when she demanded, "Why would you?"

Isiah had already turned away from the conversation and told her to "Just leave me alone."

"Don't do this to me," she remarked with frustration.

"To you?" he flared. "I said leave me alone. Last thing I want is to have an argument."

"We need to talk about why you tried to kill yourself," she said as an accusation.

"I don't want to talk to you," he made clear. "This is already becoming an argument. And it shouldn't be. It's a fucking tragedy, but you don't get that."

She spoke, "I'm not happy. Did you even think about how this could affect your family? Your dad was worried. I was worried."

"It's always about you!" he snapped. "You don't listen. You just want to yell at me without considering what I might be going through. I don't care. I stopped caring a long time ago."

"Fine then," toned aggressively, "tell me."

"I don't want to!" he repeatedly expressed.

"How can I help if you don't want to talk to me?" The question was like a slap. "I'm here now. I'm listening. Go on and talk."

"It wouldn't matter if I did," he refused.

"I'm your mother," said like that mattered.

"It's not like you have any right to say that," he bit back hard. "You haven't been there my entire life."

"I've been—!"

"What!?" He demanded a justification. "Getting your medical degree? Being a doctor? How's that going for you? Is the success everything you wanted? Was it worth giving up your son for that?"

"You wanted to live with your dad!" She harshly reminded.

"I was eight, and dad was lazy and selfish!" Isiah explained. "He let me do whatever I wanted, and I thought that was amazing. It didn't take long to realize the reason I could do anything was because he didn't care to actually be a parent. Neither did you. So, I grew up without anybody that loved me."

"If I knew . . ." she choked. "You could have talked to me."

87

"How?" He questioned. "You've been a stranger to me my whole life."

"I thought I was doing the right thing," she professed.

"You were wrong," he had to hit her with that.

Instead of letting her anger and sadness take over, she divulged her own tragedies, "You know I grew up poor. As far as I can remember, all I wanted was to escape that life. When I finally did, I was so afraid of ending up back there. That's why I threw myself into working as hard as I did. And I believed as long as I provided you with a good life, then everything would be good. But I guess that's not true. Hearing what happened almost broke me. I'm not the most emotional person, but I do love you. I thought . . . I never wanted this. And I really wish I was there for you when I should have been. I guess . . . heh . . . I'm sorry."

After a long pause, Isiah promised, "I never hated you. And I never blamed you. I love you, even if I don't really know what those words mean. But I do mean them. And I'm sorry for bringing up the stuff that I just did. I just want you to understand what I'm going through instead of being mad at me. But we always end up arguing whenever I try talking with you. Maybe because my reasons don't make sense to you or because I don't seem grateful. I don't know. But I want our relationship to get better. But I don't know if that's possible."

"Things will change," she declared, but her words were just a hope.

"How could they?" he saw no resolution.

"Come live with me," she pleaded. "I might not have been there for you in the past, but I can be there now if it's not too late?"

One year later and Isiah soon returned to Darkess Noir. There had been many options to choose from, but the one he wanted and inevitably decided on was to come back. That was the effect this place had over those who were unafraid.

Isiah's mother did not like the idea of him returning to the place she had almost lost him. However, she did not want to hold him back from his choices. Her only condition for his return to this city was that he had to attend Eversound College, which he did get accepted into.

The first day of classes began. Isiah sat in the lecture hall as Professor Oswald Rook spoke about religion and mythology from an anthropological standpoint.

A girl sat beside Isiah, one he recognized.

She spoke, "You've become rather interested in the occult ever since your near-death experience."

"Tia," he remembered after all this time. "Are you the real Tia?"

"I'm just a student," she remarked.

"How can you be?" Him referring to her blindness.

"I was able to talk with Mr. Rook before registering for the class," she explained. "I'm able to get most of the required reading in braille from the library. And he said he'll be lenient on any assignments that I don't have readings for. I just have to work with someone in class."

Isiah had nothing to say.

"Not going to ask who I decided to help me?" She teased.

"I'm guessing someone that isn't me since that's something that needed to be decided before classes started," he gave his thought-out reply. "You just want me to assume myself."

"Boo," she expressed to confirm that he was right. "Though, you should help me when I need it."

"I'm sure you know more than anybody else in this room about the subject matter," he could only imagine that to be the case if she was the goddess of peaceful death.

She smiled. Then the topic was changed, "Have you written me any more poems since you've been gone?"

"Not so many," he admitted but was content with that fact.

"I loved the last one," she expressed. "But I know the fewer you write is a good thing. Would you read the new ones to me after class?"

"Sure." He smiled at the idea.

First Day with the Dead

To fear Death is not uncommon for Death carries these three things, true uncertainty, the experience of loss, and feelings of pain. That explains the fear that many have of hospitals for a hospital is inherently tied to Death.

St. Kindred Hospital was an elegant house of mercy. Exceptional doctors worked the top floors. The sterile halls of perfect white passaged patients in and out. Rooms were filled with an orchestra of machines. The top floors of this place were where a constant battle for life was waged.

But below the building was a different world where death had won, the morgue. An iron cage elevator led down as well as a staircase that spiraled around. Fluorescent lights plastered the walls of the hall white with a haunting glow as if infused with souls. There were two doors of sleek metal in this dead end. One opened to a frigid fridge that stored the corpses. The other led to the autopsy room.

Closed and contained, the room of examination was cleaned and without clutter. A wall of cooling shelves preserved those waiting to be cut open. In the center was a slab of stainless steel where bodies would be laid, waiting for the blade. Another door led to a back office for the living examiners.

Jordan stepped out of the back room, dressed in clean scrubs and a plastic, black apron. He was ready for his first day of work.

A cold corpse of a man rested on the examination table.

Another living body stood in the room. Emilia Trime was the chief physician of the hospital. Though cutting up cadavers seemed menial for one as distinguished as herself, she often took time to work with newer staff. There were very few hires at any given time, which allowed her the chance to develop a professional relationship with those just starting. And there was rarely an influx of patients, which gave her the time to provide personal input.

"Welcome," Dr. Trime greeted in monotone. "Do you prefer being referred to by your first name or as Dr. Setly?"

"Just call me Jordan," he answered humbly. "As a coroner, I don't know if I deserve to be called a doctor. Also, I feel that going by doctor is a little pretentious."

She gave a raised eyebrow stare. "I'm Dr. Trime . . ."

Jordan immediately felt a bit awkward with his, what now felt like, a conceited comment.

". . . I'll be supervising you today. Though, I'm certain of your skill. You have a great resumé and great recommendations."

"Yeah," Jordan spoke casually. "Richard Knowns was an amazing mentor and always gave me praise. But I bet he inflated my talents."

"Maybe so," she acknowledged the possibility. "Still, I did get a look at your career record as well and was impressed. You have a curious mind and steady hands. You could have been a surgeon had you chosen to be."

"I hear that a lot." Jordan relished in the praise. "But I get too anxious working on living bodies. Then I make mistakes. Less nerve-wracking to examine the dead where I don't have to worry about killing someone."

"Sounds like you thought it through. I expect that makes you better at this work. Therefore, let's begin." Dr. Trime swept her arm as a way to instruct him to do as she had just said.

Jordan moved up to the body that awaited. He took a scalpel from off the tray nearby. The razor edge lowered to the skin, pressing and cutting barely in, but then stopped. "Who was he?" the question needed to be asked since this body had been found in his backyard.

Dr. Trime seemed put off by the question since it lacked professionalism, yet it held a degree of consideration because she was also aware of what happened. "His name is Travis Polt. There is little to say about his personal life. At least nothing inherently obvious that would have led to his death."

"Are you sure?" Jordan maintained a degree of skepticism as he began the process. The flesh was split along the collar to create an intersecting V. Then, a cut went from the bottom of the letter all the way down the stomach. The skin was spread, and bones were broken. "Nobody buries a body unless they're trying to hide it. Furthermore, just by looking, I can tell this man had been buried alive."

Dr. Trime gave a curious look as she checked the work and came to the same conclusion. However, "Having been buried alive, I would say that this is more likely to be an accident."

"Well," Jordan offered more, "there is dirt and grass under his fingernails. Certainly possible that those materials got there by being buried, but the abrasions on his fingers suggest he might have been dragged."

"Possibly those abrasions occurred from panic after being buried?" Dr. Trime considered.

"No," Jordan refuted. "He wasn't buried in any kind of container; therefore, he most likely would not have been able to move once buried."

"Foul play?"

"Seems likely but not definitive," Jordan admitted. "How does one bury a man alive without inflicting any visible injury? The only one he has is a dog bite on his leg, which we know he was an owner of. Your thoughts?"

"I would rule this as an accidental death," Dr. Trime confidently declared. "Killian, his dog, was known around the town for digging holes. Travis Polt most likely fell into one of these holes in his backyard, instinctively attempted to catch himself, was knocked unconscious by the landing, and his dog buried him."

Jordan made a quick examination and remarked, "There does not seem to be a head injury."

Dr. Trime was impressed by Jordan's thoroughness.

"Also," he needed to add, "I met the dog. Seems unlikely that a little beagle could have dug a hole deep enough for a man to fall into."

"Then you haven't really met that dog," Dr. Trime remarked. "He is well known around the town for his digging—" As she was about to make another comment, her beeper beeped. She looked to see she was being called on. "They need me upstairs. Continue your work. I'll check your assessment when I return." She then exited the room.

Jordan, freed from watchful eyes, decided to go to the back office for some procrastination. Of course, he would return to check for any potential details he might have missed. But most of the examination was done by this point, and the rest could wait. He sent a text to Oswald that simply said, 'Hey.'

No more than half a minute later, Oswald responded with an 'Aren't you working?'

With such a quick response, Jordan knew that Oswald was not busy at the moment and made a call.

Oswald answered with the same statement, "Aren't you working?"

"The examination can wait," Jordan neglected his duty. "There's not much to really discover at this point. And there are no other bodies to check today."

"Sounds slow," Oswald remarked. "Are you okay with that?"

"I'm good with getting paid to do nothing," Jordan admitted. "Though, I know you hate that for yourself. So, are you busy?"

"A little," Oswald answered. "I'm getting a coffee from the teacher's lounge right now. But I have to get back to my class in a minute."

"So, you don't have time to talk?" Jordan was disappointed.

"I have a minute," Oswald offered that time.

"Getting a minute to talk with you is more than I could have hoped for," Jordan happily accepted. "How are the students? And the classes? Any cute boys?"

"None as cute as you," Oswald flattered. "The students are great for the most part. Most actually are interested in the subject I'm teaching. Though, there are those few that don't seem to care."

"That's the worst," Jordan criticized. "I know you love teaching and love what you teach. These kids aren't giving you any respect."

"I know," Oswald agreed. "But that's what college is mostly for nowadays. A third want to learn. A third is pushed here because of their parents. And a third want that college experience, which is to say, spend thousands of dollars, land themselves in debt, and put themselves through aggravating amounts of stress so they can party on the weekend."

"I guess those ones get what they deserve," Jordan cynically approved.

"I think that, regardless of why you go to school, you get what you deserve," Oswald added a bit of positivity to the pessimism. "Now then, I have to get back. I love you."

"I love you, too," Jordan said as a goodbye and soon returned to work.

There was a moment of confusion first when stepping back into the autopsy room. Then fear followed franticly. The body was no longer on the slab. Now it was standing somehow, completely unmoving, with its back turned.

The intestines hung between pale legs. Guts were spilled. Blackened, congealed blood clumped in a poor pool on the floor. There was no way the man was alive. Jordan had no explanation, not that he could form any thought at all. What he knew he needed to do was leave whether or not there was any true problem posed. There was no desire in taking a risk.

Steps were slow and soft to keep from being noticed. But, as if in some unsettling dance of imitation, every inch that Jordan moved, the body turned. He needed to get across the room faster or else . . . But it only seemed to begin turning faster to match his pace. He was soon passed the table. But now it was looking over its shoulder, neck craned, iris jammed into the corner of the dead eye, and mouth hanging open.

Jordan reached the door, hand gripping the handle, ready to throw open his escape. But he couldn't. The fear of eyes on him left him paralyzed. There was some imposing force right behind. He had to look back. Every other part of him was in refusal. Still, his head slowly turned. He wished he had not. There was the standing corpse, fully turned around, staring directly at him.

Jordan yanked open the door and ran out. His sudden reaction had the corpse enter a sprint. He was halfway down the hall before the door almost shut. Before closing, it was hurled open with force, slamming into the wall. A heavy bang echoed. He had to look back as he ran, seeing the corpse right behind him, dead eyes locked. That fear only made him run faster. Yet, heavy, clunky steps were getting closer and closer. They seemed they would reach him. But . . .

Jordan rushed into the elevator, turning quickly to slam the iron gate shut.

The corpse crashed against the barrier, hands gripping the cage with bewilderment and yanking with rage. Though, eyes stared dead ahead.

For just that moment, Jordan had escaped. But he knew the door was not locked. Just a pull to the side would move the line of defense. Only activating the elevator would ensure his safety. He cranked the lever. The motor whirred, metal rattling, and he slowly ascended.

Empty eyes traced the lift's ascent. Then the corpse turned its head slowly to the side to see the staircase. Up. Fingers clung to the grating, arms pulling, body dragging. Slumped feet lifted and slammed, hitting each step, pushing to move.

The elevator moved slowly, not much faster than the corpse that trailed after. Jordan spun in a circle as he watched it follow him up. They went up and up and up, eyes never looking away, never blinking. Barely any distance was being put between them. Floor by floor, there was no stopping, there was no escaping.

The very top floor was reached. Only half a staircase had been made between the two. Jordan yanked open the door and rushed toward the roof access. The corpse was already up the steps, chasing down the hall, weight thrown forward, hands grasping greedily, arms swiping.

Jordan slammed against the exit. The metal door was heavier than expected and hit him back hard. The shock from his shoulder traveled through his body.

Nerves shook. Legs gave. He fell. In a panicked scrambled, he rolled over to look back.

The door hung open and, in the shadow of the hall, the corpse lumbered forward. It stared straight ahead with a fixation. And that fixation was the outside.

Once stepping onto the roof, the corpse came to a stop and stood stoic. Eyes began to roll in completely different directions from one another. Then it tilted back and forth as it turned around. Behind it was the access which it walked back toward.

Jordan was confused, relieved, afraid, and curious all at the same time. He could not move. He could not take his eyes away.

The thing began to climb up on the concrete elevation. Arms pulled, and it crawled belly over the ledge. Then it stood with shoulders drawn back as stomach distended. Arms hung loosely like ragged ropes. Face faced straight up at the sky.

What followed was some kind of decrepit display. It hunched forward, arms crossing over its chest as it slowly lowered into a fetal position while balancing on its toes. Head turned to face up again with its mouth wide open. Eyes began to bulge, bugging larger and larger until they were forced out of the sockets. From the three orifices slithered out fleshy tubes that writhed back and forth, twisting together, fusing to be one clump that pulsated and grew like a balloon.

Jordan was well disturbed by the monstrosity before him. He did not know what to do. He barely knew what was real. He had been so gripped that he had not noticed until the words called him.

"This is where you went?"

He looked to see Dr. Trime had appeared in the doorway. "Doctor?" his voice was shaky. "There's . . . a thing." He pointed above her.

She tilted her head to the side in a curious manner. To find out what he was indicating, she stepped out onto the roof and looked. She sensibly said, "Seems the body was infested with a parasite."

"Parasite?" Jordan could not believe that was what this was.

"Not common, but this happens," she assured.

"That's completely terrifying," he had to say. "Insane to even believe," he needed to add. "I'm mean, it's like something out of a horror story." None of this made sense in the world he knew. "It was like being chased by a zombie."

"It might have seemed that way, but it wasn't chasing you," she enlightened. "The parasites enter buried corpses, take over the basic motor functions, and head toward the highest point. You happened to flee in the exact direction that it intended to go."

"Then, what's it doing now?"

"That's how they reproduce. When that abscess sprouting from the face eventually bursts, spores will be released. Let's call an extermination team before that happens. Come. Stand up."

"Oh, right." Jordan had forgotten he was still on the ground. "Seriously, though. This isn't normal."

"Untrue," Dr. Trime refuted. "There are parasites like this all around the world."

Worms

Jordan and Oswald finally returned to their new home now that it was no longer a crime scene.

Jordan, staring with his heterochromia eyes of sea-foam-green and golden-hazel, judged and again approved, "Still looks nice."

"Even after the body in the backyard?" Oswald tested the opinion.

"Yes," Jordan did not seem the least bit bothered.

"And the parasites that apparently live in the ground?" Oswald challenged again.

"Gross, but yes," Jordan was able to overlook the issue since it only affected the dead, not them. Plus, they did have an exterminator come by and spray the lawn. Problem solved.

"Then let's go in," Oswald said with a smile, happy that these incidences had not scared Jordan away.

The two got out of the car. Oswald began to make his way to the front door. But Jordan, yet to even close the car door, stayed beside the vehicle as he was looking toward the neighbor's home.

Three kids were playing hopscotch in the driveway, two boys and a girl. They were relatively the same age, with the same light brown hair and fair skin. Siblings, no doubt. Everything about them was normal. What was distracting was this poem that they sang.

"I tell you to take caution and care
You must be warned, beware
And, please, don't stare
Lanky is right there

"There is no need to be shaken
You should not fear being taken
Unless you're the cause of his awaken
Lanky only seeks those forsaken

"Do not lie nor act a façade
For if you do what is outlawed
You will start to notice things so odd
Lanky is the servant of a vengeful God

"Do wrong and he does appear
You will sense him very near
His hollow eyes will begin to leer
Lanky traps you in endless fear

"Now the chase has just begun
But there is no chance you can run
And hiding is not possible for anyone
Lanky won't stop until he's done

"His elongated arms will grab so tight
They will pull you into a world lacking light
A true oblivion causes such a fright
And Lanky consumes your soul out of spite"

"What's that you're singing?" Jordan called out curiously to the kids.

They stopped their game and turned to look. Their faces brightened with the cutest smiles. Playfully, they ran over.

The girl spoke first because she arrived at Jordan first, "Your eyes are so pretty."

A boy added, "I like the golden one!"

Then the last said, "No! The green one is better!"

"Thank you," Jordan appreciated the praise. "But about that song?"

"That's the Ballad of Lanky," the girl titled.

"Lanky?"

"Yeah!" They seemed so excited as they shouted together. Then each took turns interrupting one another as they gave descriptions.

"He's really tall like a lamp post—"

"Not that tall. More like a tree—"

"Trees are taller—"

"Not the one in our backyard, and he's as tall as that tree—"

"And he's got small hands and a small head—"

"They just look small because he's so big. They're normal-sized—"

"His eyes are like black holes—"

"He wears a fancy suit—"

"Worms spill out of his sleeves and his pant legs—"

"And when he opens his mouth—"

"There's a bunch of worms in there too—"

"Oh! And he has hair. Whenever people think of him, they never think he has hair."

Jordan patted the air with his raised hands to calm the kid's energy as he spoke, "He sounds kind of creepy."

"The creepiest!" said with glee.

"He's amazing!" came more glee.

"Well," Jordan was a bit unsure how to feel about kids who loved monsters. "I'm glad you think so. Now, please, if you would excuse me, my boyfriend is waiting for me inside."

The kids seemed to sulk. Then one popped with joy, screaming, "Okay! We'll see you around, mister!" And that was the cue for them to run off back to their home.

Jordan gave a sigh of relief. Not that he hated kids or anything. It was just that these ones, in particular, had more energy than he knew how to deal with. No longer being held captive, he went inside.

"How's the neighborhood?" Oswald asked while he busily unpacked.

"Those were some happy kids," Jordan had to admit. "But also, very weird. They sang the creepiest song. I wonder where it came from?"

Back during the cold war era, when violence reigned supreme, as wars ended and secret wars continued to rage, the city of Darkess Noir was influenced by the blood being spilled around the world.

The early morning was darkened by black clouds that threatened to wash away any evidence there might be. The crime scene was located on the main street of downtown. A bold place to erect such a horror because of the frequent traffic, but that same reason was why the place was chosen. Many people had witnessed what would forever haunt their dreams. Unfortunately, none had seen the criminal. Whoever was responsible had used the pitch blackness and seclusion that dawn had provided to remain hidden and escape long before police arrived.

The victim was a woman named Jane Whitman, though she would never be recognized as who she was ever again. Limbs and neck had been pulled, skin was torn like wet paper, and the tendons stretched to be wiry cords. A rope had been wrapped around her waist, which was used to hang her body from a lamppost. Appendages dangled, moving whichever way the wind commanded as a grotesque chime.

But the most disturbing, if that could even be possible, was what was done to her face. Her eyes were viciously gouged out and worms stuffed into the sockets and down her throat. They wriggled and fell from her face, writhing in the pool of blood that was below her. There was no doubt these atrocities had been done to her while she was still alive by how the fear had forever contorted the features of her face.

The body had been taken down long ago and sent to St. Kindred Hospital. Only yellow tape and blood remained as signs that something terrible happened here. Though, those signs would be gone very soon. Hopefully, the autopsy would make up for what was about to be lost in the rain.

Detective Caeseal Wood took a drag from his cigarette and blew the smoke toward the melancholy sky.

"Anything new?" asked his partner, Detective Bonney White, a small and smiley woman.

He turned to see her making her way over, carrying two cups of coffee, one with a donut balanced on top. She handed the just coffee to him and, now that she had a free hand, picked up the donut and bit down. The strawberry frost made her squeal like a giddy child.

"You smile too much," Wood accused. "Especially around this morbid shit."

"I've gotta," she took another bite, chewed three times, and swallowed fast, "Nobody else is going to. Definitely not you. All those negative thoughts only bring more back on us. Try saying 'the crime is being solved' instead of, I'm guessing your thinking, 'Why couldn't we have already solved this?'"

"Like that actually works," he said critically.

"It doesn't matter if it works," White said, which meant that being positive was the only importance. "I can stay focused unlike you who gets so clouded by your emotions. See," she stuffed the rest of the donut into her mouth as she wandered closer to the blood splatter, "the wind was blowing south at the time the body was being lifted. The rope had been drawn over the right side of the lamppost and pulled down the left. That meant the perp had to be standing downwind of the victim. Blood traces would have landed on him—"

"None of that helps if we don't have a suspect," Wood argued. "And the pooling of blood covered up any possible shoe prints."

"True, but don't you see the speckling?"

Wood took a closer look. Speckles were in every direction, but the concentration was toward the south. However, though the spot was not bare of blood, there was a lot less in a particular segment than in most of the area. It was a sort of silhouette.

"There we have our suspect," White declared. "We find out how fast the wind might have been moving at the time and do some fancy math, we can get a rough height. Everything is coming together."

"Maybe," Wood was at odds. "But this is the third effigy, and that's not much more to go on. How many other victims do there have to be before we stopped this psycho?"

"You're not wrong," White admitted to the first part of his concern. Then she addressed his second issue, "I couldn't say for sure. But we're making progress. We will stop them. Maybe the coroner found something on the body that could help?"

"So, to St. Kindred?"

"Nope. No point going all the way there if there's no new information. And if there is, we'll receive a call. Let's head back to the station."

"Sounds good," he was in agreement.

The forensics team was informed to measure the height of the silhouette and try to determine the wind speed during the time the body was being placed.

Then the two stepped away, crossing under the yellow tape, and went to a car parked nearby. Wood took the driver's seat, cranking the window down a crack so he could blow his smoke out as they began to drive. That left White to take passenger, which allowed her to freely eat from the box of donuts stashed inside.

"You're going to get fat," Wood warned.

"Never," White declared as she chomped down on another donut. "You're going to die if you keep smoking."

"Doubt it," he defied as he took a deep drag.

His action challenged her to eat again. But he was not so childish to keep up this contest of killing themselves. After blowing the smoke and flicking the ash, he put out the cigarette and wondered, "How accurate do you think we can determine the perp's height?"

"Couldn't say," she shrugged. "Within a few inches at best. Maybe we get lucky, and the perp is really tall. That would narrow down any potential suspects. There are few people over six feet. And we know they're most likely a man since most women don't have the strength to hoist a two-hundred-pound male. You know you fit the description."

"I'm only six one," he mentioned. "Not that uncommon, is it?"

"You're not denying the accusation?" She stared with raised eyebrows.

"I'm not the culprit," he said definitively.

"I believe you," she accepted his claim. "You have an alibi. You were with the wife this morning when the crime was being committed."

"Anyway," he reminded. "The height has yet to be determined. You shouldn't be throwing around accusations yet."

"True," she accepted that she had high expectations.

"Who knows," he suggested as a jab back at her for accusing him, "I'd say that a smart, small woman could find a way to lift those bodies and set up misleading evidence."

"Now you're speculating too much," she advised instead of humored.

"Isn't it best to keep our possibilities open?"

"Occam's Razor," she presented in contrary.

"The simplest solution is most likely the right one'," he cited.

"That's the most common quote. But I was thinking, 'Entities should not be multiplied without necessity.' We need to focus on what we have, not what is possible if we want to find this guy."

"I'll keep that in mind." He popped a cigarette from the pack.

"Don't bother lighting another. We're almost to the station."

His hand remained held up for a moment as he annoyingly contemplated her suggestion. He sighed that his addiction could not be fed. Finger pushed the bud back down.

The car hit one more stoplight, then turned into the lot. They parked in the reserved spot at the back of the building. White jumped out when she could, calling back, "I'll see you inside," knowing Wood was going to stay back and smoke. He did not intend to but, being given the chance, he enjoyed a cigarette outside the car. He met with her in the office when he was done.

White was staring at the evidence board. Once Wood entered, she speculated out loud about the most recent crime scene, "I'm expecting the same rope and the same weapon were used, as well as the same species of worms. There are no witnesses just as before. The location doesn't seem to be associated with where the other victims were found, not even a hidden pattern on the map, though this is the most public so far. We could say the perp might be getting reckless. Though, I'd be speculating. Thoughts?"

Wood took a second to think since he was put on the spot. But he was not afraid to admit, "nothing."

She continued, "We've yet to find any kind of pattern. Another woman was killed, but the victims are more or less random since the first two were a man and a woman. Their ages ranged between twenties to late sixties—"

"They're all white," Wood noted.

"Yes," she recognized. "Still, even that's probably by chance. Darkess has diversity but is mostly consistent of Caucasians. Even if we were to take that into consideration, the victims' occupations and where they lived, hobbies, and love lives all differ, though not to a degree that seems to avoid similarities. The time of death and the locations they vanished from are also widely different. Even the time between the crimes is inconsistent. There. Are. No. Connections."

"Perhaps this is truly random," Wood commented.

"That's not good," White admitted. "Solving this would be entirely reliant on luck if that was the case."

"Well," Wood revised, "Think about this, the victims might be completely random, but the motives might not be. To act so viciously has to have a reason. Any normal serial killer would have moved on to the next town by now."

"I completely agree with you," White believed. "But what? What could we expect the perp to be motivated by?"

"Ritualistic sacrifice?" came the suggestion, though how serious he was could not be determined.

"The body placement," she reminded, regardless.

"That might not matter," he disputed. "Limb stretching, eye-gouging, and the worms have significance. Then the bodies are disposed of randomly, or maybe they're being placed where they can insight the most fear. This last body was on the main street. The previous was found in the park. And the first was along the highway leading into the city. These are places where plenty of people would see the bodies."

"Inciting fear, huh?" White became pensive. "I didn't consider that. Probably because I would have assumed if the perp wanted attention, the bodies would have been placed at the school or the mall. However, even though those places have a higher concentration of people, fewer people would have seen the bodies because the response would have been more immediate. If this is the case, then a lot of consideration had to have been made. Which means we could predict where the next body would show up."

"Next body?" Wood's words disdainfully pondered on her implication. "I would prefer to catch the culprit before that."

"I'm not saying we don't try," White spoke with little optimism. "But we need to plan for the worst. Let's take the time to deliberate any possible locations and place a request to have those places patrolled more frequently."

"Understood," he accepted with little acceptance. "Where do we start?"

"Wherever you want. We have a lot to look into."

The two began. Maps of the city were scoured over to search for specific locations that might fit the elements of the crime. What little evidence had been recovered was also looked over. As well as ledgers of individuals who were under suspicion. And they even delved deeper into the significance of ritualism. Hours passed. They never discovered anything actual. There were only hypotheses.

Eventually, Wood became sluggish, rolling stiffness from his shoulders, then he looked at his watch. "It's ten now. I should . . ." but he did not finish his statement.

So, "Go home," White finished for him. "You've been here long enough. I bet your wife is worried."

"Not worried," he knew. "She would have called the office if that was the case. But I shouldn't keep her waiting. Are you sure you want me to leave you on your own?"

"Go ahead," she was sure. "I don't plan on staying much longer myself. Though, if you're so eager to keep working, there might not be much to do outside the office, but you can take a few files with you."

Wood leaned back in his chair, crossing his hands behind his neck and placing his legs up on the desk. He gave more than the needed thought to the suggestion. His decision made him sigh, "No. Bringing this grim stuff home will worry Elly," his wife.

"Then go," she insisted. "I can tell you're worried to clock off because you think we might not solve this before there's another victim. But we should have time. The latest victim was discovered today, giving us a few days at the very least."

"I know you're right." He fell back into a sitting position. "I've just been wasting time worrying." Standing up and stretching followed. "I'll see you tomorrow, White."

"See ya, Wood."

Wood exited the office and soon exited the building. Across the lot, in his car, and out of the police parking lot was just as quick.

Darkess Noir was brighter tonight than usual. A full moon looming in the clear sky radiated light upon the walls of fog, turning them into spectral curtains. The entire city seemed to glow. The streets were free and clear of both shadows and people. With his drive being safe, his addiction in his hand, and a staticky radio playing barely audible music, he thought about everything.

In fifteen minutes, he reached home. Two more minutes were taken to finish his cigarette before going inside. From the foyer, he could see light spilling through the archway of the living room. There was no calling out about his return since, even with the lights on, his wife could have been asleep by now.

Entering the room at the end of the short hallway caused him a shock. A table had been broken, the couch was flipped, and there was scattered décor everywhere. The house had been tossed.

"Elly!" He screamed. "Elly!" Instinct had him charging from one room to the next. "Elly!" He called out again in hopes that she would respond this time. "Elly!" But there was no finding her.

The truth was answered by the silence. Wide eyes and clenched jaw became a tightened brow and gritted teeth brought on by rage. Fist punched a hole in the wall.

A robbery? A kidnapping? Could this be the serial killer? The only way to know would be to read the story of the scene. There was no certain answer, but plenty of obvious evidence explained what he needed to know. No valuables had been taken, meaning this was not a break-in. Whoever had invaded, definitely several individuals, had come for his wife. Though, there was still no knowing if this was random. In either case, she put up a struggle.

Another detail struck him hard, returning fear and dashing his hope. A broken clock revealed the time that this happened. She was taken fourteen hours ago. His

111

experience as a detective told him that his wife was already dead.

He would not accept that. His heart believed there had to be a chance even as his head repeated the hopeless reality. But he kept rejecting those thoughts, even criticizing them for not helping. That was when every potential disposal location of the serial killer flashed through his mind. There was no knowing if this was the serial killer, but this was his only lead. He grabbed his revolver and rushed out of the house, jumping into his car.

The first potential location was reached. There was nobody and no time to waste. He went to the next. Then the next. To the next and the next, he kept speeding toward one after another. But none were the spot.

Check them again? That would be stupid. That would waste time. What was he even doing? His actions were already a waste. What he needed to do was contact his colleagues and tell them what happened to get their help.

That idea was lost as he came upon the next location, the far end of the downtown pier, across from the farmers market, next to the loading docks. What caught his attention was a van. The vehicle itself brought up a lot of questions, along with why it was out at this time, nearly two in the morning.

He parked a block back and approached carefully, making sure to remain inconspicuous and undetected. Peering around a building that blocked the road from the water, he witnessed figures. They seemed like wandering wraiths but were soon recognized as a dozen robed individuals. Their hooded disguise only added to the emerging sense of dread.

Immediately, he blamed them. In his mind, they were too strange not to be the culprits. Gun was drawn.

He was ready to confront and question what the hell they could be doing. Before he did, he saw her. They had been obstructing his sight but, when the body was raised up, she appeared. Elly! Elly! Her limbs were stretched until the tendons tore. Her eyes had been gouged. And worms spilled from her mouth.

Wood stepped out from his hiding spot with the gun raised and gave no warning. He just pulled the trigger. The barrel flashed with an explosion. A bullet struck one of the figures in the back of the head. They dropped dead to the ground.

The others turned around. Another shot was fired, killing again. But none of the figures were afraid or surprised by the sudden violence or by the deaths of those around them. They merely began a slow walk toward Wood.

The gun fired a third lethal round. Still, they never stopped.

The fourth shot hit, and the figure staggered from the stopping power. A hand touched the wound and witnessed the blood. Yet, it did not care and continued to move forward with the rest. Another bullet ended that one's life.

Wood pulled the trigger for the sixth and final time. He was aware right after that his revolver was empty. He should have known better than to fire uncontrollably. But his anger had clouded his mind. One hand reached for more bullets as the other emptied the casings in the gun to attempt reloading.

The hooded figures recognized their chance, and they rushed forward zealously, grabbing.

He had only been able to load one round which he fired. The bullet hit a figure in the leg, but that did not stop it or the rest as they thrashed. They used their power to push him to the ground. A blunt weapon was raised and struck him repeatedly in the head. The first hit made the world skip. The second made everything blurry. Another brought black spots. Then the count was lost in complete blackness.

Wood woke in confusion. It took him a moment to recognize that he was lying on his back, staring upward. What came into his view was an endless blackness above, with pillars around extending into the pitch, and a florescent glow from floodlamps surrounding, though, the void was not in the least affected by the light.

He tried to move only to meet resistance across his entire body. Arms, legs, and even his head were strapped down. Already weak, already in pain, he struggled all the same. But the harder he tried, the tighter the restraints squeezed. He could barely move an inch.

There was no escape. A weaker-willed man, or perhaps a smarter one, would have given up. Wood would not have if he had the choice. Unfortunately, his initial struggle suddenly turned against him. The pumping of blood woke his body, making him feel the throbbing split in his head. The world spun, fading in and fading out. He began to sweat. And breath was barely. Numbness left him paralyzed.

Footsteps clambered around. He could see nobody. Only the voice reached his scattered mind.

"This night took four of our members. A price to pay to be blessed with another sacrifice so soon. Take up your arms, my brothers and sisters." Metal clattered at the command. "To you, our Dark God, Nemesis, we feed the pain of yet another victim."

Wood became wide-eyed as a sudden sharp agony was inflicted to one of his arms.

"Feed!" Cried loudly.

Another stab was done to his other arm, and he screamed out.

"Feed!" Cried louder.

More stabs followed to his arms, to his legs, to his stomach. They kept stabbing and stabbing and stabbing. He thrashed with adrenaline to no avail.

"Be gluttonous," the leader spoke more. "Be greedy. We will feed you soul after soul as we wait for the day you reveal yourself to us. Consume their pain. Consume their hate. Revel in their revengeful thoughts the moments before they fall into despair and vanish."

Hands entered Wood's sight. Gripped tightly in each was a large road spike. Then the arms came down hard. Both eyes were pierced, a shallow pierce that scraped the back of the sockets but did not puncture the brain, blinding, not killing. The amount of pain suffered had already numbed every nerve, yet fear remained. Being enveloped in sudden blackness, thrown into the unknown, left in nothing was the most terrifying. He was filled with horror. He screamed and screamed until his voice was lost as vocal cords shook and tore.

The spikes began being bashed back and forth as if the madman was playing a drum, all the while laughing manically. And as he played, the others became fervor by the bloody beating. Some continued to stab. Others grabbed hold of a limb and began harshly pulling. Tendons were stretched like wires, legs and arms made long. The intensity of violence grew quickly and ended just the same.

Malicious tools were dropped to the floor, causing a storm of sharp sounds that echoed. The speaker gave the final command, "Feed him to the pit." The others unfastened the straps, and dragged the mutilated corpse off the table and across the chamber to a vast vat. Inside writhed millions of worms. Wood was thrown in.

The crawlers wriggled, drawing his body down slowly into their realm. As he sunk, they entered his torn flesh, knotting themselves with his exposed tendons, burrowing into his eye sockets, slithering down his throat. This infestation joined them together as a host with a parasite.

Little could he argue. He was dead. His heart had stopped. His brain was black. Still, the rage of his soul branded an endless hate onto his corpse. His fury radiated even now.

This living pit slowly faded to feel more like an oblivion as the squirming motion, and slimy texture vanished. This world now felt like somewhere that was both the bottom of the ocean where all was black and the pressure crushed, and in the void of space without stars, weightless and drifting.

Something moved through the unknown as if rising from beneath. Wood felt as if landing upon a surface. He laid in the palm of power.

A voice. A voice that was not a voice, but the echo of reality creeping from every corner, *How very blind and foolish these swine are. I have been right before them this entire time, and they have never seen me. They're just bloodthirsty and happily insane. They'd be better off worshipping Korn instead of me. I much prefer those filled with rage, those sufferers of pain, those seekers of revenge. That is to say, a man like yourself. They took everything from you. Your wife. Your child yet to be born—*

There was a pulse of volatile emotion.

I see you weren't aware. Just another reason to hate them for what they've done. How much pain they put you through. Tore your body apart. Tore your soul apart. Given the chance, I'm certain you would do the same to them. I can give you that chance. Become my acolyte. Through my will, you shall enact your revenge.

116

Another force came from above, seeming to cup Wood between two cosmic hands. The clasping force created power in the center that was infused into him. His dwindling soul resurged. Undeath was granted.

Starting with fingers slowly pressing out from the surface, a desperate hand rose from the pit and kept reaching and reaching and reaching and reaching even more as the twisted, elongated limb fully extended. Gangly arm dropped, catching the edge of the vat, and pulled. Head emerged, eyes hollow black, dripping tears of tar. Mouth was barely parted in a way of sad, shocked, exhaustion. Between the small gap of his lips, a writhing movement could be seen. He rose and rose and rose and rose even more as contorted, stretched legs carried him. Worms spilled out of the stab wounds in his stomach. Feet found ground on the cold concrete, and he stood with full posture, taller than any man could ever grow to be.

The room was vacated. Only the blood-stained table remained as a reminder of what happened.

Set on the table was something unexpected, a suit. It seemed to have been fashioned from corporal shadows. The black shade was so deep that light was eaten by the fabric. The glossy appearance shifted and moved with life. And the fit was perfectly proportioned to the acolyte's new length.

A gift. Professionalism is important before starting a new job. Now, let's begin.

He dressed.

Who were they, these cultists? A store clerk. A rich mogul. Soccer moms and blue-collar men. They came from every walk of life and every social class. Only this disturbing interest in the occult was what they shared. Trying to recognize them as a group would be impossible without knowing that detail.

The acolyte had seen the faces of the cult when he was human, and the disguise was lost. Though, this new form could see far more, looking upon their very souls. He was drawn to them by the wickedness that they enacted and by the wishes of others. People wanted to see justice. And he had his own revenge to think of.

Each was visited, hunted. They could not run. They could not hide. Their souls were ripped from their bodies, leaving behind a husk deemed dead. But they were not lucky enough to be granted death. Instead, they were forced before Nemesis.

A return to the modern-day.

The three kids continued to play the games that they had been playing throughout the evening. Though, the sun was falling below the horizon, and, because of the wall of fog, it was already out of sight. The ghastly white was igniting a burning orange that made the city glow.

Their mom, Suzie, a small brunette lady, stepped out of the house, calling, "Dotty, Max, Herald. Dinner's almost ready. Time to come in."

The three briefly paused as they listened to the instructions. Together they screamed, "Okay!" not upset. Then they ran inside with much energy. Their mom was found finishing the cooking in the kitchen.

"How can we help?" asked Dotty.

"Could you set the table?" Suzie requested. "And would you boys go get your father?"

Dotty accepted her task with a nod and began grabbing dishes, utensils, and placemats.

Max and Herald ran upstairs, banging on their parents' door and shoving it open impatiently. Inside was darkness. Barely visible among the shadows sat an elongated silhouette. Head turned. Hollow, haunting eyes, blacker than the scene, leered back.

"Dinner!—"

"Dad!"

Sockets, empty or otherwise, expressed a softness from how the brow furrowed. A close-lipped smile was kind. Lanky stood with a hunch since the room was too small for his stature. Each son wrapped around one of his legs to be carried by his steps.

The family came together in the kitchen. Max and Herald let go of their captive and took their seats across from Dotty, who was already sitting. Suzie and Lanky sat at the heads of the table.

As Lanky reached for his fork, a distracting worm fell from his sleeve. Max, sitting right by, picked up the bug and returned it with a smile. His dad smiled the same, taking the worm, and tucking it back from where it came.

"So," Suzie started the conversation, "what have you kids been up to all day?"

"We met the neighbor—"

"He's so cool—"

"He's got pretty eyes."

"I'm glad to hear that you like him," she was pleased. "I'll have to go over there sometime to say hi myself. What about you, dear?"

Lanky adjusted his head in thought. There was nothing to be added which was expressed as a shrug. Facial expressions changed, and he pointed at her.

"Something else?" she read.

He smiled and nodded with a finger held up. Standing and walking out of the room, a door was then opened in the next. A moment later, an excited beagle ran into the room with a wagging tail.

119

"Puppy!" The three kids squealed as they jumped from their seats. They showed love with many pets and scratches.

"That's Killian," Suzie recognized. "We're adopting him, I take it?"

Lanky patted the pup as his way of saying 'yes.'

The One Who Knocks

Elaine Cane, always dressed in her school uniform, was a girl with boundless determination. That characteristic was very helpful in her line of work, spreading the gospel. Most youths would be broken by the non-caring world that slammed door after door in their face. But she never gave up regardless of the endless amount of failure she suffered. A strong fist in the air and a triumphant scream battled those feelings when they began to weigh.

Every day, after Booker Black Private High School let out, Elaine made her rounds. As a responsible student, one on her way to being valedictorian, she made sure to limit herself to only a couple of hours. She still needed to study after all.

Routes had to be planned to be most effective since the city was spread wide. There were the two suburban-like neighborhoods, one on the east side of downtown and the other between downtown and the west side. Then there were the many apartments on the west side. Not to mention the many colonial homesteads beyond the west side, those on top of Padlock Hills to the south, and those along the Puget Sound toward the north, with a few estates hidden in the forest. There was also the historical district, better known as the upper-class neighborhood on Topsy Hill, located south of the downtown. Then there was downtown as well. So many homes needed to be visited.

Today, Elaine wandered around Padlock Hills. She approached her first door and knocked. A man answered and showed a slight interest, mostly because she was pretty.

"Hello, Sir," she greeted with enthusiasm as she presented a black book. "Have you heard the word of Vindication?"

"Uh," clearly his interest was completely lost, and he declined everything she was offering by saying, "no," as he slowly shut the door.

"That's okay," she assured, leaning a bit so her smile peered through the crack of the door before it closed. But she could not help from sighing once the lock clicked. Oh well. Off to the next.

Another door was knocked and answered. She presented her book and began to speak, "Hello, ma'am—" the door closed immediately. Sigh. On to the next.

Another door was knocked. Then another. And another. She must have knocked on a dozen doors. But they each rejected her. She thought to give up for the day. The purple twilight had already taken over. If she did not begin returning home soon, she would be walking in complete darkness.

But her persistence had her decide to knock on one more door. Not like doing so would be much of an issue. She just did not want to end the day with only failures.

She continued making her way up the hill. Eyes were locked onto the next house that was on the top of the bend. However, to her fortune, she would not have to go so far. It turned out that there was a closer house. Where most properties were right along the paved parkway, this one had a private driveway that dipped down. The short hill blocked sight from the main road. She was only able to notice it because she was walking by on the sidewalk.

She began toward her new destination. Careful steps were needed to descend or else she might slip because of the steepness.

At the front, the door opened to her knocks. Standing on the other side was a dignified old man. He wondered, "Why's a sweet girl like you come to visit me?"

"Well . . ." she paused to prepare her line, "Hello, Sir. Have you heard the word of Vindication?"

"I couldn't say that I have," he answered with a happy curiosity.

She was made confident by his smile. "If given a moment, I'd love to share the message."

"I'd be happy to sit and listen." He stepped back as an offer for her to enter.

She stepped inside and gave an appreciative bow of the head. Down the hall found the living room. A comfortable couch was the perfect place for her to settle. There was another seat across from her meaning they could have a face-to-face dialog.

However, the old man took it upon himself to sit right beside her.

The nearness was uncomfortable for Elaine. She decided not to say anything so as not to be rude. He probably had a small personal bubble.

She took a breath to steady herself. "Mind if I read a passage to you?"

"Go ahead." He stared intently with little interest in anything other than her.

She opened the book.

He placed a hand on her thigh.

Her book snapped shut and she shot up from her seat like a rocket. "I'm sorry. I should be going."

He stood up as she moved passed him, and he caught her by the shoulders.

"Please let me go." She attempted to pull away.

He pulled her back harder to be pressed against him.

"Let me go." She tried to push herself free.

123

He spun her around and forced his lips against hers. She turned her head, face filled with disgust. "No!" He grabbed hold of her chin so she could not reject his kiss. Arms fought but were overpowered. He pushed her toward the bedroom. "Stop!" But she could not stop being dragged. He used his weight to push her down on the covers, keeping her pinned beneath him. "Let me go!" A hand went down her side, going up her skirt, and tugging her underwear down. She kicked and screamed, thrashing, throwing her arms recklessly.

"Stop struggling." He put a hand around her throat. Squeezing fingers took her voice away. And the threat of death took her fight. His other hand unfastened his pants.

Hips pushed aggressively into her. The shock left her paralyzed. The thrusts were painful. But worst was the violation. He grunted and sweat. More pressure was put on her windpipe as he neared his climax. His other hand shoved her face hard against the pillow as he stroked harder and faster. He began calling her all sorts of obscenities while insisting that she loved what was happening. That added humiliation was what he got off on. His face tightened as he finished. Then he rolled over, exhaling rough, exhausted breaths. Quickly, he was asleep.

The old man eventually awoke. How he rose from his slumber, stretching and smiling, revealed what little empathy he had for what he did. He was a true sociopath that would keep victimizing others for his own enjoyment without a single shred of guilt.

Though, there was something he did regret. Looking over, he saw that the girl was still in the bed beside him. He was surprised. His guests always ran off once he was done with them, never returning because of the shame. So, this made no sense. But, at a closer look, he knew why. Her skin was pale, practically turning blue. She was dead.

He did not mean to. Though, that was not why he felt regret. His only concern was what he would do with the body. Disposal would take more time out of his day than he wanted.

A knock came from the front door. Another visitor was unexpected, but he was not worried. He fastened his pants and went to answer.

The door opened and on the other side stood a high school girl, the very same girl. She spoke her prepared line, "Hello, Sir. Have you heard the word of Vindication?"

What was going on? Wasn't she dead in the other room?

In a flash of bewilderment, the old man grabbed her by her wrist and dragged her inside. He intended to make a demand. Impulsive panic had him strike her in the face before he said a thing. She tumbled back, her footing lost, and her head smacked hard on the corner of a hallway table. Body dropped to the floor, heavy and limp. She was dead . . . again?

A knock came from the front door.

The old man turned back around with a lost look. He approached the entrance carefully this time, almost as if afraid of what could be on the other side. Instead of opening the door right away, he peered through the peephole. The girl, the very same girl, was standing on the porch.

How? Wasn't she dead in the other room? Wasn't she dead right behind him? As he began to pull away to check, she turned to look directly at him through the spyglass and smiled as if aware he was staring.

The look drove the old man mad. He flung open the door and charged at her. She was knocked to the ground. He was on top of her. Both his hands wrapped

125

around her throat and squeezed. She needed to die. Whatever was going on would be solved when she was dead. And, without breath, she died. . . again? . . . again again?

A knock came.

The old man stood fast and turned. Cold fear and a sense of confusion overwhelmed him. Reality had shifted. He was not outside anymore. Somehow, he stood in front of the door from the inside of his house.

A knock came again, insistent.

He jerked open the door. There she was, the very same girl. But behind her was the body of her that he had just strangled. Checking over his shoulder saw the other body that had hit her head. If that was the case, he needed to know so he ran to the bedroom. There she was, her abused body still on the bed.

A knock came from directly behind.

The old man felt a chill run down his spine. The door was right behind him, just waiting to be answered. But there was no way he would turn around.

A knock came, seeming closer, sounding louder.

But he refused.

A knock came, even closer, sounding much louder, shaking his body with each bang.

But he would not turn around.

A knock came, inside his very head, shaking his brain violently. A sense of vertigo almost made him fall, and his nose began to bleed.

But there was no way he would turn around.

A knock came—

He spun around and threw open the door before the feeling that had been creeping closer overtook him. There was the girl, the very same girl. He begged, "What do you want?"

"Have you heard the word of Vindication?" she asked with the sternest expression and tone.

"Come in," he desperately offered in hopes that this repeating nightmare might end.

"Thank you," she said as she entered, stepping over her own body and taking a seat in the living room.

The old man dared not come too close, staying near the hallway.

"Allow me to read an excerpt," she pressed. Book was opened. Throat was cleared. "Law is Law. On a battlefield, honor shall receive honor. In a hospital, curing shall receive curing. In a home, hospitality shall receive hospitality. To go against this exchange, the wrong will receive all wrongdoing. An eye for an eye leaves the unjust man blind and the just man unharmed." She snapped the book shut with a surprising resonance.

The old man was paralyzed. He could do nothing as the girl stood up and began walking his way. He was almost suffocated by his held breath as she stood so close. Then she stepped right passed him without even slowing her pace. He exhaled once she was gone. It was over.

A knock came.

The old man turned around and looked down the hallway at the front door. He approached slowly, seeming to take hours to answer. His hand was sweaty when he took hold of the handle. And pulling the door open felt to him like dragging an iron slab.

On the other side was himself, a shadow form of himself that is. The old man's silhouette smiled like a pervert. It grabbed the real old man and forced their lips together in a disgusting, nonconsensual kiss. He tried to push the thing off him but could not. He struggled in vain as it dragged him toward the bedroom.

Today, another day, Elaine was making her rounds on the west neighborhood. She had received many rejections as usual but was feeling good about this next one. After having knocked, a man with a small scar on the bridge of his nose had answered and was giving an intense look.

"Hello, Sir," she presented, "Have you heard the word of Vindication?"

Oswald leaned in, very curious about the book, "I haven't. Is this some kind of religion?"

"Well, not a religion per se," she explained. "It's a teaching."

"Something occult?" he assessed.

"Well . . . I guess you could say that," she hated to admit.

"Is this something that originated from here?" He kept probing.

"Yes," she answered. "Though not formally introduced to Darkess Noir, Vindication is as old as the town itself. It is believed to have been started by a select few members that colonized this land."

"That old?" He was in disbelief. "Was this like a secret society?"

"Maybe back then," she assumed. "But it's kind of died out. I was hoping to re-enlighten people."

"Why?"

"You ask a lot of questions," she could not help responding since this was the fifth.

"And I hope you can answer them," he remarked. "I'm a teacher at Eversound College. And I teach anthropology with a focus on religion and mythology. So, I am very much, in fact, interested in hearing about the Vindication."

"I'd love to tell you all about it," she said with great enthusiasm.

"Then come in," he offered, and she accepted. "Jordan, we have a guest."

Elaine left Oswald and Jordan's home feeling rather positive. Oswald had shown more interest than any other person she had spoken to. They discussed the deeper and more complex topics that she often had to avoid otherwise people were left confused. He even asked her to talk in his class and offered her free credits if she wanted to take his subject when she entered college. As for Jordan, he was kind and charismatic. Though some things went over his head, he did enjoy hearing about the mysticism. There were times he added his own colorful ideas on how Vindication could work, which were worth honestly considering. What a good experience.

Visiting my neighbors? The world echoed.

Elaine turned her head to see Lanky hidden beneath some shadows as he stood on his porch, smoking a cigarette.

"I thought this place looked familiar," she said as she looked around. Then, looking down at her book, she answered, "They're a nice couple. Unfortunately, I don't think they'll be joining, but I'm happy to have someone who really listened, even if from an academic standpoint."

They do seem like good people. Though, I do get this strange feeling from them. Anything you noticed?

"No," she said, then, so as not to talk about them behind their back, quickly switched the subject, "I heard you adopted Killian."

He is an acolyte of Nemesis like us. Honestly, though, I just wanted to give him a good home.

"I'm glad to hear. Have you been busy at all?"

129

Not so much. The city has been quiet this year. Though, that probably means something is coming. But let's talk about that another time. It's rather late. Aren't your parents going to be worried?

"Oh crap!" She just noticed that the sun was down. "What time is it? Are the buses even running anymore? I'm so grounded."

Just tell your parents what happened, and you should be fine.

"They don't get what I'm doing," she explained. "They don't argue much because I get good grades, but they think this is just a 'phase,'" put in quotations using her fingers.

Well, how about a lie?

"That doesn't seem right," her sense of righteousness argued.

Eh, what they don't know won't kill them. My wife will drive you home, and you can say you were tutoring my kids.

"I . . ." she was hesitant to agree but did, "can do that. But I won't be making a habit of it."

Let me go get her.

"Wait," she stopped. "Did I ever thank you for what you did for me?"

Whenever we see each other.

"Well, thank you again."

Flesh Bound

It was an early morning with no need for an alarm. Jordan and Oswald slept in for a few extra hours on their shared day off, Jordan more than Oswald. Oswald was not one to waste the a.m. and rose from bed a bit after nine, fingers pinching the scar on the bridge of his nose as he rubbed the sleep from the corners of his eyes.

He kept himself busy with simple chores, putting items away that were out of place, washing dishes left in the sink from the night before, and taking out the trash. Around the middle of the hour, he began cooking breakfast for the two of them and brought the meals up to the room.

Jordan was woken by the delicious smell, giving a "Good morning" before yawning. When his heterochromia eyes of sea-foam-green and golden-hazel blinked away his tiredness, he wondered, "What you been doing?"

"Breakfast?" Oswald said as the answer and as an offer.

Jordan handled the plate while slowly adjusting to a sitting position. "Thanks." He took a bite to get a little energy before asking another question, "What should we do today?"

"Why don't we check out downtown?" Oswald had the idea ready.

"Sounds good to me. When do you want to go?"

"Whenever," Oswald showed no preference in the time.

"Don't put that decision in my hands," Jordan stressed. "I'll end up procrastinating. Five hours will go by like that before I realize we should have left. Then we'll have almost no time to do anything."

"Alright then." Oswald smiled since he knew Jordan's tendency to put things off. He decided, "Let's finish eating, and we can head out. And I was thinking we walk to downtown since it's not that far, and it looks like today is going to be sunny."

"Sounds good to me," Jordan liked the plan. "Now let's find something to watch while we eat," and they put on a show that they both enjoyed.

After finishing the morning routine, they stepped out of the house dressed in their casual best. Hands were held as they walked side by side during their calm stroll without worrying what others might think. And there seemed no need to be concerned at all in this city as others, who were also taking advantage of the weather, waved kindly to them. Today would be good as the temperature was warming and the people were welcoming.

The first interest that would truly begin their exploration of the city appeared to them rather unexpectedly. They had not even left the neighborhood when they found the sign stapled to a telephone pole. Made of cardboard, the black, blocky letters read, 'Garage Sale.'

"Want to go check it out?" Jordan suggested.

"Could be fun." Oswald agreed with a "why not?"

"You said you wanted to go downtown," Jordan answered the hypothetical question with his actual concern.

"We'll get downtown eventually," Oswald explained. "I really just want to see what there is to do around here. So, let's do this first."

"Then we're off," Jordan declared.

They continued along, going in the direction the sign pointed, finding another sign and another direction. Searching for the garage sale became a scavenger hunt as they followed the arrows this way and that way for a couple of blocks. They knew they had arrived when they found a driveway full of tables.

The modest arrangement had a variety to choose from. Jordan and Oswald chose to look around separately due to their differing preferences. As Jordan perused a section designated for music, Oswald looked through boxes of books.

Of the books, separated by genre, Oswald focused on those of fantasy and horror. A few hardcovers were appealing but not that special. Most were well-known titles of popular authors, things he had already read or already knew he had no interest in. Only one stood apart from the rest as it was untitled and seemingly very old.

He was intrigued with the small, thin book on a professional level. The covering was like leather that seemed to remain alive even after the tanning process. The texture felt soft and tugged with friction as he traced his thumb. And there was a natural warmth permeating. However, that made dating the item difficult. From what he could tell, cloth was used as a binding material which meant this could very well have been from the eighteenth century.

So curious of this finding, Oswald needed to read.

Julian Howard was a terrible man from the day he was born, for when he was born, his mother died. Let it be known that one should not normally blame a child for the death of their mother when their mother dies while giving birth. But if you ever knew Julian Howard, then you would know he would have killed his mother because she was a woman. Oh, how Julian Howard hated everybody, but none more than women.

Most believed Julian Howard's hate came from his insecurities toward his own appearance. How he did have an

133

unfortunate appearance that often-caused strangers to stare. His back was hunched, his fingers were fused, and large moles covered his body. But those deformities barely compared to how twisted he was on the inside. Let it be known that a person's appearance does not make them a terrible person. Nor does one's appearance make them hated by others. Maybe judged at times, but not hated. But for Julian Howard, he always blamed his appearance for why he was hated and not the fact that he was a terrible man.

The town of Darkess Noir did pity Julian Howard for his deformities. Even with the need for everybody to contribute, those in charge only asked Julian Howard to do the bare minimum, that is to say, even less than what a child would be responsible for. But he did barely that. Let it be known that his failure to work was due to sheer laziness. Even though he might have been deformed, he was not crippled in any way. Julian Howard could have done more and chose to do less. Maybe people would have liked him had he been less selfish.

But Julian Howard was the most selfish, filled with an entitlement undeserved. He demanded praise for what little work he did. He acted as if he was owed by the town instead of, as a citizen of the town, responsible for the town and the people's wellbeing. He would holler when he was not thanked for fetching a single pale of water. He would yell if not told he had done a good job gathering wood. He would scream if not shown admiration for shoveling dirt. How the people got fed up with Julian Howard.

Soon, nothing was expected of Julian Howard. Nobody wanted to deal with his behavior in exchange for what was barely considered his help. That left him a parasite on the small town, living on the outskirts to do as he pleased while still being fed, clothed, and sheltered. Yet, he acted as if he was being shunned. He cursed the people of Darkess Noir for exiling him as if they had done so because of his appearance and not at the fact that he was a terrible man.

In self-isolation, Julian Howard began committing his true misdeeds. He enacted unfounded revenge on whatever small animals had the misfortune of crossing his path. He killed squirrels. He killed rabbits. He killed cats. He killed dogs. And he was not kind about doing so, beating them with hammers, stabbing them repeatably with crude tools, and sawing off their legs all while they were still alive. Such sick suffering excited Julian Howard.

One day, a young woman by the name of Marry Fouster was scavenging the woods for herbs. She was alone when Julian Howard found her. He approached with a smile because she was pretty. He complimented her on her looks and how she worked so hard, and how that made her an amazing person. She thanked him. Then he asked if she would be with him. She refused him. That did not make Julian Howard happy. He had been so nice, he believed, and that meant, in his mind, he was owed something. Of course, it was his looks he blamed for her rejection. He accused her of being a terrible person for not giving him a chance just because of how he looked. He proceeded to call her fat. He called her ugly. He called her a whore.

Marry Fouster was uncomfortable and afraid and tried to leave. But Julian Howard forced her to the ground and raped her. No amount of crying or begging stopped him. If anything, he was more excited. He began smashing her face in with a rock while abusing her until she died. But, if anything, her death made him more excited. He continued to do terrible things to her body even after her spirit was gone from this world.

Julian Howard had no remorse for what he had done. He felt his actions were justified after how Marry Fouster was so rude to him. And, as compensation for having been treated so badly, he felt that he deserved to keep her. So, he took her body back to his home and hid her under his floorboards. Truly awful things were to be expected. Whenever he felt the mood, he would drag her out for his pleasure. Julian Howard was a truly disgusting, terrible man.

Sadly, Marry Fouster would not be found until after Julian Howard was dealt with. If she had been, then much of the suffering would never have happened. Her family would have found some form of closure much sooner. As well, Julian Howard's other victims might have lived, and their families would never have grieved. The town would never have felt cursed, and the people never made to feel afraid of a fictional beast they believed stalked the nearby woods.

Four women went missing in a year's time before the depravity of Julian Howard came to light. And he was only exposed because of his own indignation. As he wandered through the town of Darkess Noir, he happened upon Anna Potter, who he had been eyeing for a long time but never had the chance at. He took this encounter as a sign in his favor and engaged overly eager with a shower of praise and compliments, which was understandably off-putting. Then he asked if she would be his, and she refused. He became aggressive as he always did, saying how he was a nice gentleman and how she was rude for rejecting him because of his looks, which was not the reason. He yelled profanities as he escalated and escalated to the point where he struck her with all his might. There were others to witness this assault, and they were quick to get involved before anything worse could happen. After that, Julian Howard was never allowed in, or anywhere near Darkess Noir.

How Julian Howard hated Darkess Noir. He blamed them for treating him unfairly, believing it was because of his appearance. He had only lashed out at Anna Potter for how rude she had been by rejecting him. He felt that if everybody else knew what it was like to be deformed, then they would have shown him sympathy. Instead, they made him an outcast. Let it be known, none would have shown him sympathy even if they had been deformed. Julian Howard was outcast because he was a terrible man.

Only a few days of living as a hermit and Julian Howard was already desperate. Life was not easy, having to take care of himself. He was capable of getting his own food and starting his own fire but making shelter and finding water proved to be impossible tasks. He never had to do either back in town, only now realizing how much he relied on the house he had been given and the well he was allowed to freely use. At this point, he could only wander through the woods searching for a cave where he might sleep, or a stream where he could drink. What he found was a large bolder scrawled with demonic symbols.

Julian Howard was drawn to the dark imagery and dared to touch the surface of the stone. A black goat appeared perched on top. He thought he had found his next meal. But, to his surprise, the goat spoke for it was a demon. What it wanted was to make a deal. In exchange for the man's soul, a single wish would be granted. Julian Howard jumped at the opportunity. He made many considerations, that of revenge, or to be given a woman, but he settled on what was expected and wished to be attractive.

Julian Howard, with his newfound appearance, decided to return to Darkess Noir, fully expecting a gracious welcome. Let it be known that never would have happened had he appeared before the people. But Julian Howard ended up arriving during the middle of the night because of his ineptitude, or perhaps devilish luck was on his side.

While the residents slept, Julian Howard wandered the streets. He wondered who he should see first so that they may praise him for being attractive. The person that came to mind was Anna Potter. He truly believed by appearing before her, she would feel foolish for having rejected him when he was ugly and would beg to be his now that he was not. But, when Anna Potter answered the door, she was paralyzed by fear. Julian Howard may have no longer been deformed, but he was still Julian Howard, and that terrified her to no end.

Julian Howard pressed uncomfortably close to Anna Potter the moment he had the chance. Instead of his usual fake flatter, he took it upon himself to assume her thoughts, saying that she must feel stupid for rejecting him the first time. Then, as if a kindness, said that he would still allow her to be his as long as she devoted her entire existence to making him happy. But she did not want that, and even knowing what may come, denied him again. He was baffled. Then she told him to leave. Julian Howard became enraged, forcing his way inside to rape and kill her.

That night, Julian Howard went to three other homes expecting to be pined after now that he was attractive. But each time, he was denied because the women knew him to be a terrible man. And each time, he would rape and kill them, and kill their families had they any living with them.

Julian Howard did not understand why these women did not want to be with him. He had always been a nice gentleman, and he was now attractive, so it made no sense. His immediate thought was to blame the demon, thinking that it had lied to him and he was still deformed. But he had seen his own reflection and knew that not to be the case. Therefore, the women must have been entirely at fault.

The continued arrogant ignorance of Julian Howard was what led to his capture. He did not even attempt to flee after his crimes as he believed the townsfolk would be on his side. But when the bodies were discovered in the early morning, and he was seen proudly parading around the town covered in their blood, there was no disputing he was responsible. Julian Howard was taken into custody and brought to execution on the same day.

Oh, how truly terrible a man Julian Howard was. He would never take responsibility for his faults. Even in the face of death, standing on the gallows, a noose around his neck, he blamed everybody else. He first blamed the women for his actions. That caused an uproar and demand for him to recognize that what he had done was wrong. Instead, he accused the townsfolk of being jealous of him. Let it be known, nobody cared that Julian Howard was attractive. They knew him to be a terrible man, and he was hung for that reason.

However, Julian Howard did not die when the rope went taut. Nor did he die after hanging for most of the day. It was determined that he had become immortal alongside being made attractive. To him, he felt recognized by some higher power and boasted endlessly. He demanded that the townsfolk worship him or else suffer his wrath. But the people were fed up with Julian Howard and decided to challenge the limits of this immortality.

Who is to say if Julian Howard is still alive? The possibility does exist. But what kind of life could he possibly have without agency. His body fat was turned into candles. His bones were shaped into tools. His skin was made into leather. Organs were harvested. Meat was fed to the animals. If Julian Howard does still live, he lives in suffering for the rest of his existence. So is the just fate of the most terrible man.

Oswald raised his eyebrows at the final lines he read. The story seemed to be a work of fiction, yet there was an implication that this book was bound in the skin of Julian Howard. Oswald examined the exterior again but could not find any obvious indications. Still, possibly because of placebo, the feeling was warm and fleshy like that of a human.

Jordan approached, holding a few things that he found. "Look at these candles. They have this design where, while they melt, the wax reshapes into another candle. Supposedly, they can last forever. In fact, the guy said these were from the eighteenth century. I don't know if I believe him, so I wanted you to look at them."

Oswald was shocked by what Jordan was presenting after what had been read. He looked at the candles and evaluated, "Those are most likely from the eighteenth century. But we're not keeping them?"

"Why not?" Jordan was surprised that Oswald was not interested in the historical items.

"They're not made out of wax," Oswald explained. "They're made out of fat. Possibly human fat—"

Jordan immediately dropped the candles in disgust. "Really? Did people do that back then?"

"It's possible but not that common," Oswald admitted.

"What makes you think these are human candles then?" Jordan needed to know.

"Something I just read," Oswald held up the book.

"And what is that book?" Jordan was concerned about what the answer could be.

"It might be made out of human skin," Oswald said honestly.

"That's fucking gross."

"You have no idea," Oswald agreed. "Now, I am going to buy these," the book and the candles.

"Why on God's Earth would you want them?" That made no sense to Jordan after learning what they were.

"Don't worry," Oswald assured that they were not for personal reasons. "I'm going to bring them to the school for research purposes."

"Okay," Jordan could understand. "That's fine. Because there was no way I was going to let you keep those on the nightstand or something."

"Never," Oswald swore. "These things make me uncomfortable, too. Though, I'm surprised you're reacting this badly to them. You do work on dead bodies every day."

"Yeah, normal dead people," Jordan declared the difference. "Not things made out of people. That's just . . . just . . . just . . ." no comparison. "We're going to drop these off at home before we continue walking around, right?"

"Yeah, let's do that."

Eye of the Artist

The most beautiful woman made of oil and ink. The muddled colors flowed like a river, adding life to the stillness. The curls of her dirty blonde seemed to bounce. Her pale blue dress cascaded down her body to show her shape. She was looking over her shoulder, even arching her back a bit as if desperate to see what was behind her. But whatever there maybe was unknown. Her gaze was focused on something not contained within the canvas. Was she afraid? Was she curious? The answer had been left up to interpretation.

Pinned on the frame was the first-place ribbon.

Next was another painting of that very same woman. She sat on a chair, clearly posing. She smiled, clearly forcing the smile. What she wore tried too hard to be glamourous. Everything about the image felt fake. But that was the point. The image was to be a commentary on modeling itself.

This one achieved second place.

The third-place painting was unlike the other two. Hyper-realistic. It was not of the woman but of a woman. Black hair like a pharaoh and the smug look of royalty made her a princess. But that pretty face was attached to the body of a creature so distorted and deeply disturbing. It was piggish with a bloated belly while the torso withered away and exposed breasts sag like water balloons. Gangly legs were spread, and between them was a large, gory gash, that of a wound, not a vagina.

Sophia Nightingale, the woman who was imaged in the first two paintings, could not help but be focused on the third.

"Remarkable, is it not?" Spoke an older gentleman that had snuck up next to her.

The woman eyed him for a moment, quick to recognize him as the host of this party. Every posh person of Topsy Hill had been invited, from politicians to thespians. A few extended invites were even sent to the even higher class that lived on the outskirt mansions with the full expectation of being ignored. The entertainment for the night was a display of art by local artists to be judged and sold.

"It's . . ." she searched for the right word, "enthralling."

"As are all of Jack Solomon's works," the artist was named. "He sees people's truest selves, their monsters. That model is Sasha, and I swear that's the perfect depiction of her. Her face is painted because she lives off her image, but underneath she's just a used-up whore. We all know it. I've been with her myself a few times. Cost me a car but . . . well . . . old men like myself have needs after all. Though, with what's going on between those legs, I'm guessing she was abused which explains a lot. I heard she was right mad once she saw the painting. But what did she expect?"

"I wouldn't know," Sophia answered with an off-put tone.

"My apologies for being so forward, Miss Nightingale." The host shamelessly admitted, "A part of me hopes you would like a car as well. But I know you are not like Sasha. You are the muse to most of the artists in Noir because you have dignity. I do apologize for this old man's dirty thoughts."

"You are forgiven," she accepted with hesitance. "And I take your lecherous words as a compliment."

"Thank you for showing mercy," he appreciated. "So, what are your thoughts on Jack?"

"I've never met the man, so I couldn't say." However, she still had an opinion to share, "Though, based on his work, he's either insane or a genius."

The former part of her comment was a true surprise. "You're the most famous model and he the most famous artist in this town. How have you two not crossed paths?"

"I guess we swim in different circles," she responded with nothing more to add.

"True. Jack is not a snob like you and me. Fine wine and silver platters never interested him. When he comes to these parties, he prefers to work instead of mingling."

"How does he work, exactly?"

"Have you seen my mural, Miraged Land?"

"That is an exquisite piece," she remarked. "Are you saying he is the artist? It's nothing like this portrait work."

"Maybe not. But it's still infused with his insanity. Ever wonder why the only color used is red?" Before a possible reason was given, he answered, "He used his blood. Cut his wrist and smeared the wall, without my permission, mind you. But I am an avid collector of his, and he knows. A part of me wants to believe he was giving me a gift. Wishful thinking, I know. He only ever does what he does for himself."

"Is he here by chance?"

"What chance?" That was a dumb question. "You're looking at his submitted work."

Sophia was quick to recover, "As an oddity, I wouldn't know what to expect of Mr. Solomon. He is as likely to submit his work by mail as he is to bloody up your walls."

"You're right about that," the host acknowledged. "You should go looking around. He should be easy enough to find if he is still here. I must excuse myself anyway. The auction is about to begin."

"I hope the rest of your night goes well," Sophia added kindness to her goodbye.

"Hope to see you around, dear."

Sophia made her leave to the back of the room. She was not that interested in finding the eccentric artist, Jack. She just wanted to get as far from the conversation as possible. But a new interest caught her before she left, the call of . . .

"For the piece, 'Her of Babylon,' by Jack Solomon, the starting bid is set at a hundred thousand."

That was an exorbitant amount to start for a third-place painting— "A hundred and ten" came as an immediate challenge. More followed to raise the price further. The final price ended at eight-hundred and seventy-six thousand dollars.

The first and second place paintings went up for sale next and earned less.

Sophia could not help but remark, "What's so special?," to the stoic stranger with glasses standing next to her.

"I don't honestly know," the stranger admitted. "I guess rich people are just as disturbed as the rest of us. You take the disgust of human nature and call it fine art, and they'll eat it up."

"Well, you're here," she remarked. "You must be rich like the rest?"

"I am," he answered. "Eight-hundred and seventy-six thousand dollars richer in fact. But I already have everything I'll ever want. The money will end up in one charity or another. I personally don't care."

"Wait?" Sophia was suddenly caught off guard. "Are you Jack Solomon?"

"Just call me Jack," he used his preference as his answer, "and you are?"

"Sophia Nightingale."

"Who?"

She was taken aback and repeated, "Sophia Nightingale."

"I don't know who that is," he repeated with the same disregard. But, to give her some benefit of the doubt that she was a worthy model, he took off his glasses and gave her his opinion. "You have an interesting look. Something I might be interested in. But? No, no. Somethings missing."

"Missing?" That felt like a personal attack. She needed to know, "What exactly?"

"Nothing I could explain," he answered as he put his glasses back on.

"Am I not as disturbed as your other subjects?" She remarked.

"You very much are," he said with certainty. "Beneath that beauty is someone far more damaged than most. But that's what makes things annoying. It's as if you're so close to being complete." He pinched his fingers near each other. "However, you aren't. Which begs the question, why would I want to paint an incomplete picture?"

Sophia held her composure rather well. However, the beating by words did cause a flare in her head. Anybody would be angered by the insults. But that emotion was a defensive reaction to hide her sensitivity. She also felt a knot in her chest, a deep sense of sadness for having been both unveiled and disregarded. She took a step back. Then excused herself to the bathroom.

On a downtown street corner stood a monster. In place of skin was a hard shell, round and layered in a way that looked like bulbous fat. Holes covered this bleached flesh. From the orifices emerged tubes of wriggling tissue that slid over its own body as if cleaning the surface. Quite the parasite. And a prideful one at that with the

146

crooked horns that stabbed out its skull. In its hands, a sign was held up that read, 'Ignorance.'

Jack put on his glasses.

In the place of the monster was just another monster, but this one was wearing the form of a man. He was old and white, a bit heavier set, with a permanent frown. The sign he held up said, 'God Hates Fags!' Truly a self-righteous parasite.

"You haven't painted anything in the last week. That isn't like you. Is your proso . . . prosi . . . pro, so, pag, nosia? Face blindness getting worse?"

Jack turned to look at his agent, Claire Pontain. Then he shifted his attention to the blank canvas in front of him. He placed the image of his mind, that thing outside, on the empty white in hopes that it would stick. But Sophia Nightingale appeared instead.

Ever since that gallery party, he had not been able to produce any meaningful work. That was because every time he tried to paint a subject, she would always take over his train of thought. He was aware she was what he actually wished to paint more than anyone else at the moment. And yet, he could not paint her, for he could never be satisfied. Any attempts to project her on the canvas failed to meet expectations.

So, this cycle repeated throughout the day. After failing to come up with a fitting display of Sophia, he would take off his glasses, and people watch from his perfect vantage point. His studio was on the main street, on the second story, above a café. Plenty of traffic came and went.

He took his glasses off again and returned his stare at the man, the thing. This would be the perfect time to paint. Such a beautifully horrible subject was just outside his window. Yet— Glasses were shoved back on his face.

147

"I can't seem to get Miss Nightingale out of my mind," he admitted. "And, prosopagnosia. Surprisingly, you said it right."

"Really?" There was enthusiasm in Claire's utterance. Not about being right, well, a little bit about being right. But she was more excited to hear that her artist was interested in a model. He had already become famous using amateurs. If he worked with a professional, there was no doubt his creation would exceed everything else that came before. "What did you see in her?"

"An angel," he stated.

"That . . . That is nothing like what you usually paint."

"One that has fallen into the truest suffering and despair," he completed his explanation.

"Never mind," Claire redacted. "That sounds exactly like what you would paint. Should I call her agent? We can set a time for you two to meet?"

Jack knew he needed to paint Sophia, regardless that she was incomplete. Perhaps that was the catch. Or maybe he would be able to finish the painting once he started. Of course, those were just excuses and hopes. But something needed to be done or he might never paint again.

He said, "Yes. If she's willing."

Sophia looked upon a vast painting framed on the wall of the home of a colleague of a friend.

The image was of a young church choir. Most of the boys, though lacking uniqueness, perhaps due to the fact they had not developed character yet in their young lives, held a certain innocence. Features were smoothed away by glowing skin that made them more alien than angelic. Above their heads, the shining light seemed filled with dreams of a future that still had hope. But their perfection only made the dismal entities around them far more noticeable. Seven of the boys were not so innocent. Their skin was withered and rotted, pulled tight over their skulls to be like masks of their former selves. Above their heads loomed a similar shadow that wrapped arms around, bearing down weight that made each crumble just a bit. Then there stood the true form of the shadowed figure where the priest would be standing. The monster grinned a sharp, toothy grin. Forked tongue stuck out in a hungry lust.

"His work is remarkable," Sophia admitted to her friend's colleague, a wheelchaired woman named Bethany. "But the subject matter is so dark. How come he's as famous as he is?"

"I would not say that he's famous," Bethany corrected. "He is certainly popular, especially here in Noir. There is a sort of cult following held by the elites of this city, myself included. And we pay top prices to compete for his work. But others outside the city are often unfamiliar with him and don't tend to be interested. That's why he placed third even though his work sold higher."

"Are the elites of Noir really that much more interested in this disturbing stuff?"

"It is less about a preference for disturbing material and more the stories and magic behind them," Bethany explained. "You see, this painting already has a dark implication, but it's based on a truth. Pastor Cornwall, the one depicted as a monster, had been molesting those seven boys who are depicted as lost souls."

"Painting about traumatic events is rather tasteless," Sophia could not help voicing her contempt.

"The thing is," Beth revealed, "this painting was made before the allegations arose."

"Are you saying Jack knew about the abuse?"

"I wouldn't say he knew," Beth clarified. "But he could see something was wrong. He has a natural instinct for witnessing people. To him, people's darkest sins and most painful insecurities are worn on their sleeves. Though, some of us even believe he has a supernatural ability that lets him see the monsters that we really are."

"Superstition does sell," Sophia jested.

"Well, certainly it sounds outlandish, but in either case, if you see his paintings and then meet the people he painted, they are the exact same, metaphorically speaking. Such talent is remarkable. Does that worry you?"

"Why would I be worried?" Sophia worried.

"If you choose to model for him, he will reveal everything you've tried to hide. Even the things you're hiding from yourself. To see that reflection would be terrifying."

"Or enlightening," Sophia thought positively.

She knew a lot about herself, all her pains and insecurities, the madness that put her on the edge of completely falling apart. She still remembered her past, which turned her into a contradiction, into a person that craved and needed love to live yet was incapable of loving others. She understood a part of her liked being left alone because then she could not be hurt, nor could she hurt those around her.

Or was that a false depiction she created as an excuse for her actions? Maybe she did not know herself at all. But she wanted to. If she had the chance to see herself, her true self, then maybe she could get the answers needed to fix everything that was wrong. If there was anything wrong with her at all.

Jack could show her her soul.

Jack sat on a fold-out chair as he continued to stare at a blank canvas for the last hour. Every time he attempted to project the image of his mind onto the empty white, parts seemed unfinished or just wrong. Trying to force something resulted in the thought shattering like glass. Trying to slowly apply the idea became demoralizing as it would always fade to nothing. From there, he would look back at his subject, Sophia.

A hundred times, he instructed her to change her position. Again and again, he altered the scene around her with new props, removed props, changed the lighting, had her wardrobe adjusted, and altered her make-up. But nothing was working.

To Sophia's credit, she was a professional. During the endless recasting of herself, she never complained. She did not even make suggestions or ask any questions. She let him direct her completely.

Eccentrics were chaos-driven and ever-changing. A good model needed to know how to be patient, which she had been. Though, what made being patient even easier was her need to see his vision come to life.

Unfortunately, her strong motivation made for an even stronger disappointment.

"Leave," Jack ordered.

"What?" Sophia was caught off guard. She hoped and assumed that this must have been part of the creative process. However—

"You're worthless," he cruelly answered. This was not a joke. As he had said a thousand times in his head, 'she was incomplete.' "There is nothing I can do about you. It's annoying, like trying to complete a puzzle only to find that pieces are missing. How do other artists actually consider you a good subject?"

"Let me—" she wanted to give an excuse.

"You're empty inside, and I can't paint nothing," he hissed.

Empty? Nothing? Was that the answer? Such a terrible answer was worse than anything she expected. She pleaded, "You don't mean that?"

"Get out of my sight," he ordered. "You've already wasted enough of my time."

So that was the answer. Then what was the point?

Tears began to form in the corner of Sophia's eyes. She abandoned her pose as she stood up, remaining still on her feet for a moment as if to maintain her composure. Her things were grabbed up and clung to tightly. Then she left the studio like an unstoppable force.

Claire entered the room a bit after with a disappointed look. "You made a girl cry."

"I make you cry all the time," Jack argued away guilt.

"I signed up for your bullshit," she explained. "Miss Nightingale didn't."

"I'm pretty sure she did," he rebutted.

"Then I guess it's her fault for not being prepared to deal with your impossible expectations?" She intended her question to be rhetorical.

"You're exactly right," he did not hear her words that way.

There was a second of silence.

"Damn it," he suddenly blurted.

Claire jumped a little from surprise. Then she felt a sort of confused relaxation. Was Jack feeling remorseful?

"She walked out still wearing my dress," he complained.

Claire became deflated. That made more sense.

Jack stood up. "Come along. Let's go pick it up."

"Very well, Mr. Solomon."

The driver parked in front of Sophia's home on Topsy Hill. Clair looked to Jack to say something as they were slowing. He did not wait even a moment and got out of the car as soon as they had come to a stop. That felt rude, sparking agitation. She jumped out of her side to quickly catch up to him.

Intercepting him, she demanded to know, "What are you going to say to her?"

"I'm going to ask for my dress back," he responded flippantly and pushed passed.

She caught up in two steps and matched his pace. "Perhaps try an apology?"

Jack came to a stop.

Was this thoughtful consideration?

"The door is open," he remarked as he pointed a finger lazily.

Claire sighed. Of course, that was the reason. Wait? "The door is open?" She looked to see what he meant by that. The front door of the house had been left completely ajar.

Jack began walking again, entering straight inside.

"You can't just do that," Claire tried to explain from outside the house.

He did not listen and ventured even deeper, uninvited. The décor was beautiful, if not a little bland. Too much white and too much beige. But the red caught his eye.

In fact, he entered a standstill as he looked intently at what he had found. Curtains had been drawn but in a haste, leaving a slight slit for the sun to sneak in. The scene was illuminated while the surrounding shadows became contrasted and darker. There was a bottle of wine, mostly full, on the small table for two.

153

Accompanying was one glass, nearly empty. Lipstick stained the rim. Sitting in the chair at the table was Sophia. She slumped ever so gently as if asleep, still in the perfect white dress. One arm remained on the armrest, and the other hung over the side. Both wrists had been cut, having bled a lot, and were still bleeding a little.

Then Jack removed his glasses for an even clearer look. His eyes grew wide with elation. This was the perfection he wanted. True despair.

"Oh my god!" Claire screamed. "We need to call an ambulance!"

Jack was awoken from his reverie by the outburst. His gaze shifted over with a disappointed furrow at the thought. Then, after a ponder, he said. "No."

"What?" Claire was staggered.

"Get my supplies," he responded.

"Are you serious!?" She yelled, deeply disgusted at the thought.

"Yes." This was no depraved joke. This was just depravity. But he had his reasons. "This will be my most amazing piece to date."

That alone was enough to convince Claire. She was a morally positive person, but as Jack had always known by looking at her, she gave in to pressure easily and had a greedy side. If this was to be his greatest work, she would sway herself to go along. And . . .

Without any argument, she returned to the car. The trunk was popped. Stashed away were paints, canvases, and whatever other items would be needed. His supplies were always close at hand in case inspiration struck spontaneously.

Jack set up his easel, arranged the colors he would be using, and decided on the brushes that were best suited. Then, before beginning, he demanded, "Privacy."

Claire left with no difficulty. She did not want to be there as he defaced the once most lively icon, Sophia Nightingale.

Jack was left alone to his work. Two hours were spent capturing the tragic reality. Then another was spent looking over the image. Half of his brain worked to understand the very thing he created, how nothingness could be defined so completely, how emptiness was filled with so much in an endless depth. The other half considered improvements, where to shade, where to shift the vision. But there were no tangible answers and nothing more to be added.

For protection during transport, he wrapped plastic around the canvas first, followed by a tarp, then bound the whole thing with twine.

Claire was on the front steps smoking what had to be her fifteenth cigarette. No doubt the stress was getting to her. She had not even noticed how much time was going by. It all felt like a slow creep that ended the instant Jack stepped out. She was quick to strip the ash, ready to get out of here.

He handed her the masterpiece and instructed, "Bring this back to the studio."

"What are you going to do?" She asked.

"Call the cops," he informed. "Explain the situation."

"That's unlike you," she could not help remarking.

"Don't worry," he offered a contradicting comfort, "I'm not being compassionate."

Sigh. That sounded about right. So, she got back in the car.

Jack pulled out his phone and dialed nine-one-one.

155

Claire stepped into the studio with a heavy cloud over her head. Being compliant in the situation was eating at her psyche. Whatever Jack had seen could not have been worth the abandonment of ethics. Certainly, this was not the right decision. But there was no real knowing if that was true. At least not without seeing what had been painted.

The police heard Jack out and let him go. Certainly, his actions were deplorable, but they did not go against the law. His lawyer explained, whether by photo or through the use of paint, taking a picture of the deceased was not illegal. As for the trespassing allegation, that was disputed by the fact that the front door had been left open, and he was checking on Miss Nightingale's wellness. The only accusation remaining was, 'was this murder?' Of course, this being a suicide would be determined eventually and, instead of waiting, bail was posted.

As Jack rode back in the car, as stoic as always, the thoughts that made him feel such a way were entirely about his masterpiece. 'Despair,' as it was rightfully titled, might have been even greater than the other two pieces he had already made. No doubt he knew what it was capable of if it was anything like the others, which it most definitely was, but he was not certain of the extent of the power. He would have to test it at least once on a bystander. Then he could stash it away before any significant effects occurred.

But who would he get to look at the painting? That question had already been answered.

156

Jack discovered yet another tragedy once he arrived at his studio. One of the glass displays had been broken. Right beside the vandalism, lying on the ground lifeless, was Claire in a pool of her own blood. Her throat had been slit. She held a jagged piece of glass with bits of flesh stuck on the uneven edges. And his newest masterpiece was no more than a few steps away, having been unveiled.

He crossed the room, covering up the painting once more, and placed it in his secret storage beside 'Fury' and 'Obedience.'

The police were called again. Their questioning lasted far longer this time. It was hard to believe this to be a coincidence, discovering two suicides on the same day. Of course, they would be proven as such eventually. And, again, not wanting to wait until then, another bail was posted.

The news spread throughout Darkess Noir, distorting to something less believable and yet becoming closer to the truth. 'The demon-eyed artist created a killer painting that drove any who looked upon the work to commit suicide.' Rumors like this tended to ruin artists' careers due to the mockery or because they were taken as fact. But, in this city, Jack only seemed to benefit.

Bethany wheeled into the studio, finding Jack wandering around, looking upon his own work. She asked, "Can I see the painting, 'Despair?'" Her words sounded exhausted, as if speaking was an exercise.

He turned slowly to her with concern in his eyes, explaining, "It has unique properties."

"I believe the rumors," she was well aware.

157

"Is this what you really want?" He needed a second confirmation.

"I have been bound to a wheelchair since I was your age," she began her pitiful reasoning. "Now I'm haggard and old. I have no kids to speak of. My only legacy is my work and oh how work has become dull. The only thing that has brought me joy has been your collection of art. I have relished in the disgust that you depict of people. To know that we are all very much the same has given me comfort. But age persists, beating me down every day. If I could look upon a masterpiece of yours, well, then I could die happy."

"I'll ask again, are you sure?" He seemed to be dissuading her. "I have begun painting again. If my work is important to you, wouldn't you want to see what's to come?"

With absolute certainty, she spoke, "I don't know how much longer I'll live. I don't know if I'll ever get to see what is to come. Maybe I see the next and the next. But eventually, I won't see the next. And I'd also miss out on seeing your true masterpiece. I'd rather go out on my own terms. And what better way is there to die than to look upon your greatest work? My wish is to see art that completely compels me."

"Very well," he accepted the answer. "Let's go over the paperwork," to avoid liability and earn compensation.

Jordan and Oswald looked over the curation with every emotion between deep consideration and complete disgust.

"It takes a real psycho to paint like this," Jordan remarked. His heterochromia eyes of sea-foam-green and golden-hazel often had to look away.

"There is something masterful about the work," Oswald said in support of, him staring intently at the work down the bridge of his nose with the small scar.

"How so?" Jordan asked sarcastically with a pompous tone, along with a fake smile and upturned hand.

"You have to admit the paintings are good regardless of how dark the subject matter is," was Oswald's answer.

"Well, I couldn't paint like this," Jordan admitted, rebutting immediately after, "But I'd never paint any of this even if I could."

"Says the person that cuts open dead bodies," Oswald commented.

"Dead or alive, a body is human. This," accusing the paintings, "is distorted horror far from anything human. Have you seen anything like this in your studies?"

"Other than of Lovecraftian work? No," Oswald admitted.

"Well, that guy was crazy," Jordan bad-mouthed. "So are you. I guess only crazy people can understand this stuff."

"Really?" Came the question from behind.

Both Jordan and Oswald turned around to find a stoic man standing there, holding a pair of glasses. His eyes were transfixed on Jordan.

"I'm Jack Solomon," he introduced. "This is my studio. These are my paintings."

"I'm sorry," Jordan felt embarrassed and a little ashamed for talking behind someone's back.

"Don't be," was Jack's way of assuring no offense was taken. "People that know me would all agree that I'm crazy. In fact, I'm a high-functioning sociopath. So, you're not wrong. Though, I have an eye for people, and I'd say

159

you're rather crazy yourself. A very unique kind of crazy. Do you mind if I paint you?"

"What?" was asked to everything that had been said. But, after a second, Jordan thought about this chance to model and found himself kind of excited. This Jack being a sociopath really did not matter. There was already some suspicion that Oswald might be one as well. So, as long as nobody was being hurt, did it really matter? That made answering easy, "Sure. I mean, why not?" though, some consideration needed to be made, "You don't mind, Oswald?"

"Not at all," he answered. "It's our day off. These random experiences are what we're looking for."

So, for one hour, Jack painted.

The image born was of the young man sitting on his knees, almost in a daze, head lulling to the side, eyes of pure green barely open. Another him, this one covered in scales, horns sprouting from his brow, his eyes a radiant gold, sat in a similar position while wrapping arms around the first. Where flesh met flesh was knitted and fused, bonding them together forever as two separate beings that were wholly one.

"How weird," Jordan described, having expected himself to look a lot more disfigured like the other paintings but having not expected two versions of him that contrasted each other.

"You can keep it if you like," Jack offered. "Though, I rather like the piece. I'll pay you ten thousand for your services instead."

"Ten— Ten . . . t— ten thousand!?"

"It would sell for more if you found the right buyer," Jack confessed. "Personally, I don't intend on selling it if you sell to me. It is rare that I find a subject that I actually like to see. Your right to say these people are disgusting," referring to the paintings. "But yours has a beauty to it. Something I can appreciate above monetary gain."

"We'll take it!" Jordan accepted right away. Then he looked to Oswald in case this was the right decision.

Oswald shrugged since he really did not have a say. The painting was not his, after all. Though, for comforting assurance, he did add, "I don't think we'd have time to find another buyer anyway, so I think the offer's good."

"We'll take it," Jordan repeated.

"Let me write you a check and I hope you two have a wonderful day."

Sea Salty Tears

The day was beautiful with a bright sun in the sky, which seemingly banished the fog from the city. Though, looking far out in any direction, there was still a hint of the mystic wall. However, what was usually grey was now illuminated pure and white, more like clouds. This transcendence shifted the very feel of the atmosphere. No longer was one trapped in deep uncertainty but ow stood upon a mountain of glory and grace.

Jordan and Oswald stepped out of the art studio with smiles on their faces as they basked in the warm weather. This was their first day off together, and they honestly did not expect such a nice day to exist here. This felt like a sign that those past problems were far gone.

They would use today to explore. By getting to know the city, they might feel more at home. For all they knew, this could be the place they spent the rest of their lives.

Already downtown, they continued with their window shopping. Buildings were old but refurbished. The streets were craggy yet comfortable. The people were kind while being somewhat odd. This place came from history but was not afraid to move forward with change.

Jordan and Oswald got tea at a quaint café, bought a snack from a food truck, and picked up a few knickknacks from several local gift shops. Then they checked out the science center, headed over to the farmers market, and made their way back up the boardwalk. Quite the busy outing and it was barely the afternoon.

With time to do more, Oswald pointed out a restaurant situated on the pier, aptly named 'Bay House,' and asked, "Hungry yet?"

Jordan looked at the establishment with consideration as he touched his stomach. Never one with a big appetite, nor the biggest fan of seafood, he said, "No. I'm still full from the veggie dog. But if you're hungry, we can."

"We can wait a little longer," Oswald recommended. "Eat around six or something back at the house."

"Sounds good with me." Jordan smiled at the suggestion.

"Until then," the motion of hands directed attention to what was beside the restaurant. Down a ramp attached to a dock was a small vendor. "Want to rent some kayaks?"

The smile Jordan wore gently shifted to the look of uncertainty as his gaze stared out over the water. He was used to swimming in lakes and rivers, but this was unsettling ocean water. Still, on a day like today, the water was kind of clear and had a sparkle that made the green surface seem emerald. He said "Okay," reluctantly.

The two made their way down, discussing which they wanted. Jordan liked the yellow because it would be hard to overlook once on the water, and Oswald had no preference. Jordan also wanted a double-seater so they would not get separated, and Oswald still had no preference. Then Jordan reconsidered the color, but Oswald made the commitment since he knew how indecisive Jordan could be.

However, "I'm sorry" was what the proprietor of the kayak stand had to say. "I just rented out my last one. And, before you ask, these others are reserved for a group that will be here in the next fifteen minutes. If you want, when someone finishes, I can hold onto the kayak, and you guys can come back in like an hour."

Jordan and Oswald looked at each other in shared contemplation. They shook their heads at the same time.

"No, thank you," Oswald voiced their decision. "We'll come back another day."

They turned away and Jordan asked, "What do you want to do with the rest of our day now?"

"Let's just relax at home."

Samantha and Jude paddled out on the calm water, enjoying the scene that unfolded around them. Darkess Noir was truly a beautiful place. That fact was indisputable in the middle of the Puget Sound. Forests surrounded, with tasteful buildings on the water's edge, and Mt. Rainier was visible off in the distance.

Samantha leaned back and rested her head on Jude's lap.

"This is peaceful," Jude felt.

"Sure is," Samantha agreed. "The warm sun. The cool air. And that ocean smell."

Jude exhaled out his nose at the sarcasm. "Not everything can be perfect. Well, not everything except you. You're perfect." He leaned down, and the two kissed, smiling back at each other.

"You're perfect, too," Samantha returned the compliment.

"I'm far from perfect," Jude remarked. Then he rolled to the side, out of the kayak, splashing into the water. His head popped back up with a laugh as he cleared his hair from his eyes. "See, I smell like the ocean."

Samantha looked petrified. Urging, "Please get back in the boat."

"You should jump in," Jude counter proposed. "It actually feels refreshing."

"No." Samantha was shaking her head at the thought. "What if there's something down there?"

"There is. We call them fish."

"I mean like sharks." Samantha reminded, "This does connect to the ocean. So, please get back into the boat."

"Okay," Jude agreed, not wanting to worry her any longer.

As Jude pulled himself back on the kayak, the thing tilted. Samantha had a second of panic. It seemed they were about to capsize. But that was just her anxiety expecting the worst. There was nothing to be concerned about and everything settled without incident.

With the fear over, Samantha's feelings first became relief, then they became modest disgust. "Your clothes are all wet."

"Doesn't bother me," Jude remarked.

"Are you sure?" Wet clothing was always something that Samantha could not stand feeling on her body, so she could not understand how others were not as bothered.

"I'm sure," Jude guaranteed. "But we can go back if you want. I don't think there's much left for us to do out here anyway."

"It's only been thirty minutes," Samantha was not sure about returning early. "I don't want that whole hour we rented to go to waste."

"Then let's find somewhere to paddle to." Jude spied around for anything interesting. What he spotted was a little lump on the horizon. "I see an island . . . or maybe just a rock that away," he pointed. "We should check it out."

"I know I just said I wanted to use more of our time, but do you think we'll have enough to go over there and come back?"

"They said they would charge us extra if we went over our rent time," Jude explained. "I'm okay paying extra if we get an adventure out of this."

"Well then, let's go."

They made their way over, bobbing up and down on the small wakes that passing boats created. As they got closer, the object grew to be more than a rock but not much of an island, being little more than a mound that rose above the surface. They made landing on the barnacle and algae-covered stone, Jude jumping out to drag the kayak ashore so that Samantha could get out without having to get wet.

"Watch your step," Jude cautioned. "The ground's pretty slippery."

"This is kind of cool," Samantha had to admit as she planted a foot and almost immediately lost balance. Luckily, flailing arms saved her from falling.

Jude chuckled at the display before sharing the sentiment, "There is something fun about standing on a thing in the middle of the water."

"It's like we're adventurers who just discovered a new land," she joyfully gave a metaphor.

"Exactly," those were the words. So, "Let's see if there is anything interesting to find." Together they began making their way to the top.

Not much stood out at first, with everything being grey and green. However, with a closer look, the pools of water trapped on the plateaus of stone did offer something content. Each was a habitation having a sandy floor, decorated with pebbles, sticks, and vegetation, and populated by tiny organisms, crabs, and fish. A small world that was enough for them. Nothing uncertain. Nothing out of place. Just a comfortable slice of life.

That comfort contrasted completely with what was found at the center. "A sea cave." Both were fascinated by the ominous discovery. Bore into the stone was a perfect circle leading down into absolute darkness. Uncertainty was the only thing that was certain within. What horrifying possibilities, what potential treasures, what lost worlds that could be down there caused anxious curiosity.

A hot, exhale of air expelled from the opening and was followed by this very subtle, near inaudible, high-pitched echoing wave.

"Think anything lives in there?" Jude wondered.

"Maybe ghosts," Samantha played.

That led to the next thought, "Do you think people died down there?"

Samantha entered deep, concerning thought. Such a tragedy did seem possible. That possibility gave her a wave of goosebumps as her fear rose.

"No," Jude answered his own question when he noticed how distressed Samantha had become. He rationalized, "If anyone had, the city would've sealed it. So, you want to go down?"

"Do you want to be the first to die down there?" Samantha presented the consequence.

"I said nobody died," Jude retorted. "Plus, I'll keep you safe."

"Well . . ." she was still hesitant.

"Come on," he pressured. "We're on an adventure."

"Okay," she settled.

"Awesome," Jude expressed as he took the lead with his phone out and flashlight mode on.

Entering immediately presented an obstacle as the sloped ground was covered in a thin layer of slime. Feet had to be carefully placed on notches to keep from slipping. There were plenty since the cave walls had a bulbous texture.

Several feet down opened into a wider space that, though the ground was lumpy, it had leveled out. Jude and Samantha swept their phones to see around them with no success. Their lights could not illuminate anything too far ahead.

The air churned once more, a little stronger. The sound repeated, a little louder. Both came from further in.

"Creepy," Samantha stated. "How deep do you think we can go?"

"They usually don't go too deep," Jude answered, aware that his comment would have them venturing further. "Let's keep going until we hit a dead end."

They stayed close together as they began walking into the black, the flow of air pushing and pulling the darkness. The floor squished underfoot, and water dripped from above to break up the unsettling silence. The cave was larger than expected and took a surprising few minutes to reach the back. There they found another descending passage.

"Further we go," Jude said as an action and not a suggestion before beginning his descent.

"Are you sure about this?" Samantha asked in an urge to turn back.

"We'll be fine," Jude said with assurance.

Samantha slumped her shoulders and sighed, knowing she could not leave Jude on his own.

At the bottom, they found another cavern. There was still no seeing the walls with the lights, but the area felt smaller for no explicable reason other than instinct. Perhaps claustrophobia was beginning to cause some paranoia.

Then, a more audible wave of high-pitched sound echoed through. All other ambiance was overwhelmed.

Only seconds passed for the hum to fade away. Mute was left in the wake.

A drip of water returned the world to normal.

Samantha moved close to Jude and took his hand.

"Are you scared?" Jude teased.

"Unsettled," Samantha admitted. "Anybody would be."

"Not me," Jude boasted. "I guess I'm just braver."

. . . or senseless.

They continued and discovered yet another descent at the back of the cavern. But this was a plummet, not a slope.

"Looks like the end of the—"

High-pitched and louder than before, the words were swallowed by the sound that faded as suddenly as it had appeared.

"I wonder what—"

The sound blasted again, even louder, then fell away. Bodies were left trembling.

"That's getting—"

The sound was back with even worse force. Ears rang. Head hurt.

"Alright, let's—"

The sound sounded. And sounded. And sounded.

Both were forced to cup their ears. Samantha looked at Jude and screamed words that could not be heard. There was only the sound. Loud and on repeat. Every other noise was lost.

And then the sound ended.

"What the hell!?" Jude yelled in frustration more than anything else.

"Let's get out of—"

A ring interrupted Samantha. Both were perplexed for a moment because it was a different ring than what they had been hearing. The realization hit that

169

one of them was getting a call. Jude looked to his cellphone to learn it was him.

"Could you be quiet for a sec," he ordered, then answered with false enthusiasm, "Hey, baby. What you calling about? Did something happen with your appointment?" A pause. "I'm sorry to hear." Another pause. "Oh, I'm just with a friend. I didn't think you'd be done this early. I can come back." Pause. "Okay. Love you, too."

Samantha slouched in a defeated pose while eavesdropping on the conversation. She hated the secrecy, more so being the secret. But she wanted to be with Jude because she had convinced herself he was not just playing her. Though, subconsciously, she was aware that she was the other woman.

After Jude ended the call, he looked at Samantha, rolling his eyes at her accusatory posture. "I told you things are complicated right now. But you know I love you."

"It is complicated," Samantha confessed. This was not the best time or place, but things had to be made clear, or nothing would change. "I've been waiting to say this. I guess I've been waiting for you to finally end things with Zoey before I told you—"

"Told me what?" he interrupted her potentially upsetting information with a rising tone.

Her sneer explained she was getting to that and she just said, "I'm pregnant."

"What is this about?" He accused angrily.

"This isn't about anything," she defended. "It's just that you said—"

"Why are you trying to ruin things right now?" He reflected the blame while giving excuses, "I have a lot to deal with. I can't just leave Zoey. Her father died a couple of months ago, and she is still a wreck in private. And we're still living together."

170

"Sorry for her," Samantha halfheartedly apologized. "I didn't intend for this to make things more difficult."

"Well," he pressured, "what are you going to do?"

"About what?" She began to glare in response to whatever he was getting at.

"The baby?"

"What are you implying?" Her look intensified to that of disgust. "That I get rid of it?"

"Well, yeah." He was not even hiding his intention. "This could ruin everything."

"Ruin everything for you," she specified. "You said you were going to leave her. You said that months ago. That's why I haven't mentioned this up until now. I didn't want to pressure you. But I did expect you to leave her and this to be a happy surprise."

"I wasn't lying—"

"Fuck you!" She rejected any further excuses. "You're lying right now. This child wouldn't scare you unless it puts all of your bullshit at risk—"

Jude reeled back and shoved. The action was entirely involuntary. His panic was rising, and he did not know how else to deal with the situation. He knew immediately that what he had done was wrong. But there was nothing he could do now as he watched Samantha fall backward into the hole, her face turning to shock.

The blackness grew thicker after every second of the drop. The bottom was hit. Everything became an even denser darkness that did not exist in the conscious world.

The high-pitched wave screamed. Samantha was woken by her ears being pierced. Her head filled with vertigo for many reasons. Eyes squeezed to subdue the pain. Body rocked back and forth to calm it. Neither helped.

171

Hands began to fumble around in the black. Her phone was found right by, covered in mucus but working. Just picking it up illuminated the enclosed space as the flashlight mode remained on.

Slowly looking around, Samantha discovered herself at the bottom of the pit. She stood up shakily and grabbed at the wall, thinking that she could possibly climb out. But there was no finding a grip on the slim cover surface. Even so, she tried and tried with no success until absolutely certain. That did not mean she gave up. There had to be a way to escape.

Checking around once more noticed a circular seam on the wall. It was as if an area beyond had been sealed off. The task seemed impossible and was proven to be as she pushed the barrier that did not budge to her strength. However, the seam chose to crack open. Water rushed through the gap and began filling the tunnel.

Momentary fear left Samantha frozen. Then panic hit. She screamed as she grabbed at the wall again. She screamed for help, but there would be none. She was going to die.

Wayward teens walked the abandoned railroad tracks that ran along the water's edge, joking and smoking.

One came to a stop at the sight of something unexpected on the beach. He called the others to look and make sure he was not just seeing things. When the rest of them came over, they saw the same thing. There was the body of a drowned man.

Samantha woke again, bobbing in the open water. Kelp folded over her body like many arms with no ill will. They, in fact, seemed to be holding her above the surface to keep her safe.

She breathed a sigh of relief to see the sky once more. This felt like a dream, and a part of her thought that it must be. There was no explanation for how she had gotten out of the cave. All she could remember were invisible hands along the walls, a force pushing her from behind, and just blackness. And there was that song, that voice, so soft, so kind, so beautiful beyond compare. The high-pitched wave might have berated her when her head was above the water, but when submerged, it spoke.

Following the recollection, she listened to the water once more. There was no song or voice, just the empty hum. But that was overtaken by the sound of churning. Head turned to see a boat, reading 'rescue' on the side, coming toward her.

From above, to the point where the people were no more than specks on the Puget Sound and the boats not much bigger, a silhouette was so very clear. In the body of water rested a sleeping giant.

Haunted

Deep in the evergreen of Darkess Noir, a lone mansion stood in seclusion from humanity. A once beautiful structure, whose beauty still remained in some twisted form, had long ago been abandoned. The walls were decrepit, many of the exterior panels in a state of decay and left crumbling away, while the no longer white paint was blotched by mold and peeled apart. Each window was boarded shut long ago, the wood now rotten and nails now rusted. The roof had many missing tiles and certain sections had collapsed. This husk was the remnants of Lorain Manor.

None knew what happened to the affluent family that had once lived there. Not a body nor a crime scene was discovered when authorities came searching. Everything was very much undisturbed. Though that made the circumstances far more disturbing since, not only were the eight members of the family missing, their staff of twenty had vanished as well. No explanation was ever determined for how twenty-eight people, several with families and loved ones of their own, disappeared without a trace. And attempts to find answers eventually came to a halt as those that went looking also disappeared inexplicably. The property was soon rumored to be cursed. No longer did a single soul dare enter and the mansion was left to the wilderness.

Nowadays, all were barred from entry, kept off the land by a surrounding twelve-foot, red brick barrier. The only possible entrance inside was through the iron gate. However, both man and nature never wanted the way to be open again. A thick chain and creeping vines intertwined between the bars to seal this place forever shut.

Though the day was cloudless, the sky was not blue but bleak and colorless, the sun shining pale. The atmosphere melded seamlessly with the ever-present wall of fog creating a grey ocean that the world was falling upward toward.

The time was nearing noon when two white vans drove over the stony road, pulled up to the rusted gate, and parked.

Zack, an obviously arrogant man, stepped out from the driver's seat of the leading vehicle wearing a shit-eating grin. He approached the gate with an unnecessary swagger. The ground crunched beneath his feet with each step. He stood before the gate as if having all the answers.

One hand touched the metal bars. The feel was rough and brittle. Running his fingers broke loose small pieces of iron flakes.

Taking his other hand from his pocket, he brought out a knife. The blade was switched in a smooth, show-offy motion. Then he firmly held onto the bars as he placed the knife in between the gate, at the top, and ran the blade down. The edge caught on the very first vine. He began to finick with frustration as he tried to saw vigorously through the fibrous plant, everything shaking and rattling, more dust and metal flakes falling over him like filthy snow. With little success, he placed the knife behind the vine and yanked towards himself. It ripped and the blade heaved at his face. He stumbled back.

The passenger door popped open and nice and ordinary Richard stepped out. He called across the short distance, "Need a little help?"

Zack looked back just to flare his frustrations. Then he returned to his efforts alone. He made sure to make clear, "I don't need your help, Richard."

Zack took five more minutes to cut through a second vine. Richard sighed but did nothing other than continue standing where he was. Another ten minutes for Zack and he had finally wacked away the weeds. With a heavy push on the gate, one side opened slightly before becoming jammed, the other remained unmoved, and then there was the fact that a chain still locked everything shut. He growled.

Richard chuckled and asked, "How about now? Need Help?"

Zack rolled his eyes and yielded, smiling insincerely and calling, "Fine. Get up here."

Richard strolled over with a bolt cutter in hand. He severed a link in the chain which clattered to the ground. Together they then pushed open the iron obstruction. The hinges popped as the rusted seal broke. The gate creaked like a scream and scraped over the gravel, churning the stone pebbles and kicking up dust.

As soon as there was an opening, the second van sped through.

Zack, in an overacting fashion, dodged out of the way even though there was no need. He screamed with tension hidden under false joy, "Assholes!"

The popular Melody leaned out of the passenger window and taunted, "Meet you there!"

A gravel road offered the way to the mansion, cutting miles through light forestry with pillars of leafless trees on both sides. Eventually, a vast courtyard was reached. The road wrapped around a great fountain that stood a story. From there led steps of stone to a pair of massive, wooden, double doors sealed shut by locks and chains.

They parked and everybody piled out. The three newcomers, Eve, Kyle, and Steven, along with Robert, the most industrious of the original crew, began taking equipment out of the back of the vans and started setting things up. Zack, Richard, and Melody stood around to talk about how not much had changed since last they were here, while Roseanne stood apart from the rest. Not that she was excluded. She was just the most passionate about the work, already holding a camera in hand as she filmed the outside scenery.

A close-up of the fountain captured the image of moss and mold covering the exterior. The channels were clogged, stopping any function or flow. What little water that had not drained or dried was left murky and brown with parasites as the only inhabitants.

"We have returned to the infamous Lorain Manor," Roseanne narrated, panning from the flavor décor to the mansion. "Nearly three years have passed since us Haunt Hunters conducted our first investigation into the disappearances—"

"Roseanne," Zack interrupted her monolog. "Glad to see you're taking initiative. But let's wait until everything's set up before we start filming."

"Come on," she disputed as she pointed the camera at him. "This is the raw stuff. Behind the scenes is what sells the legitimacy."

Saying "Maybe" was his way of agreeing with the idea before ridiculing, "But what we need, at the very least, is to open with something more interesting than a panoramic of the scenery," which was only because he did not come up with the idea.

"Then what would you suggest?" She snarkily asked while still filming.

"How about a close-up of me, in front of the doors, explaining the history of the mansion," he thought himself clever with that suggestion.

"Well, I think all of this is going to go into the final cut," she said otherwise.

"I get the final say in what makes the cut," he objected.

"It's a team effort thing," she reminded. Then patronized, "Though, it's not like you know how to edit, or promote, or read lines. All you do is take credit, Mr. Boss Man. Anyway, this is our sequel, remember? We already explained the history at the beginning of our first documentary. Doing that again would be redundant."

"You think the audience is smart enough to remember this place's history?" He mocked.

"Glad you have so much respect for them."

"Then what would you suggest?" he challenged.

"We recap what happened the last time we were here," she recommended.

That was when Robert barged into the conversation, "How about you help instead of waste time?"

Zack glanced over and commented, "Looks like you're already finished."

"He's right, though," Roseanne was in agreement. "We should stop wasting time. Let's get the footage we need and add whatever intro outro afterward. We planned to be done before dark."

"Alright, alright," Zack accepted. "Everybody, get a camera. We're heading in."

"How do we get in?" Eve asked.

"The front door," said so condescendingly. He proved this by walking up the steps, pulling out a key, and unlatching the locks from the chains. Then a push opened the door with no effort. "We had keys made for the last time we came here. Of course, they were going to work. The place has been abandoned for decades. Nobody's going to change the locks. Now, let's go."

The eight filed inside. Apprehension mixed with their enthusiasm as just stepping one foot in the foyer felt uneasy. They panned their cameras across the room to capture every detail. The floorboards were decaying, wallpaper was peeling, and dust layered over everything.

"Alright," Kyle began jokingly, "so this is when we split up, right?"

The original crew members glanced around at each other.

Melody was the one to say, "Actually, yeah."

"I wasn't being serious," Kyle stated hoping that would undo the idea.

"We want to get as much footage as we can," Roseanne explained.

"Plus," Zack added, "it adds tension to the content."

"I thought this was about finding closure?" Steven, one of the other newbies, remarked since that was supposedly the reason for this second excursion.

"Sure," Zack's tone said otherwise before he openly admitted his real intentions, "But we want to keep our audience entertained. We'll be separating into three groups. Myself, Melody, and Kyle. Roseanne, Richard, and Eve. And Robert and Steven. Each of you newbies will be with us veteran members so you don't have to worry. And you two," referring to Robert and Steven, "seem brave enough to be the smaller group. There shouldn't be a problem."

"Well . . ." Eve was hesitant.

"I guess . . ." Kyle tried to be confident.

"That'll be fine," Steven said in complete acceptance. His display of courage was enough to convince the other two.

Kyle decided, "Yeah, it's fine."

And Eve was in agreement, "I'm good."

"Now that we're ready," Zack brought the meeting to an end, "Team A," smugly hovering his hands over himself, "my team will be investigating the first floor. Team B, Robert's, will be on the second floor. And Team C, you know who you are, you got the third floor.

We'll meet back up right here in the next hour or two. Understood?"

"Sounds like a plan," Robert said for everybody.

And they separated.

Roseanne walked in the front with an eagerness to film everything. Her camera was practically affixed to her face as she looked down hallways, into each room, and at anything of interest. But the captured footage was quick to disappoint as she expressed, "Sad that we couldn't do this at night like we did last time."

Eve shakily exhaled as she watched a spider skitter along the wall. "This place is pretty creepy already. And I half believe the rumors are true. I don't know if I would want to be here at night. Who knows—" Thwack! sounded the heavy impact to the back of her head that left her paralyzed like a statue. She was not aware of the ax sunken into the back of her skull. The only thing she knew was something terrible had happened. Then, when the weapon was pulled out from her head, her life ended immediately. She fell limp to the floor.

Richard knelt beside the body, using the ax as a crutch.

Roseanne leaned in with the camera still filming.

"This is so exciting," Zack exclaimed. "To think we get to do this again."

"We could have done this again whenever we wanted," Melody clarified.

"Sure," Zack agreed as dismissively as possible, "But we had to go through the whole grieving process, or nobody would believe us about what happened."

"This really is just for the camera, isn't it?" Kyle presumed after hearing the former remark. Now that he was no longer concerned, he questioned the legitimacy, "there really aren't any ghosts or curses?"

"This investigation is for way more than the camera," Zack assured. "This is a passion."

"A pleasure," Melody added.

"I can tell," Kyle understood and continued to assume, "But none of this is real?"

"I couldn't say if ghosts or curses are real," Melody admitted. "But this is real. We did lose a crew member the last time we were here. There was all that news coverage and police investigation."

"I guess I do remember that," Kyle recalled with lingering doubt, "But I thought it was fake."

"How could we fake that stuff?" Melody defied.

"True," Kyle recognized. "Then what did happen?"

While Kyle was focused on Melody, Zack swung the ax from behind. The edge hacked into the side of Kyle's neck, tearing open his throat and knocking him to the ground but not killing him. But before he had time to do anything more than crawl, another swing to his head finished him off.

Zack had a pleased look. "This guy really did not know when to stop asking questions. But I guess he got his answer."

"Funny," Melody remarked to the distasteful joke.

Steven and Robert went along in silence. Neither was really the talkative type making whatever footage

181

they filmed eerily quiet. That begged the question of why they would be paired together.

The two entered a torn-down room like all the rest, Steven first with Robert right behind. Steven crossed through to the exit on the other side, filming aimlessly without any commentary.

Robert grabbed an ax stashed beside the door, inside an umbrella holder. He readied for the kill, approaching, ax raising. Immediately before he swung, there was the sound of a sharp pluck. Robert felt a force pull across his torso, dragging him off his feet. He was thrown backward, crashing into a window. The glass and wood boarding broke as his body was launched out of the building.

Steven turned around mere moments after the phenomena. He rushed to the window and looked out. The sight was brutal.

Robert did not suffer a fatal fall. Instead, his body had landed on the spikes of a fence that surrounded the exterior of the building. He writhed in agony, gargling blood as he tried to lift himself off his skewer.

"Everybody else should be done by now," Richard determined. "Let's go meet up with them."

"You go on without me," Roseanne waved him away. She was so fixated on scanning over the body with her camera to take in every detail and preserve this precious moment. Leaving now was not wanted.

"That's not how this works," Richard reminded. "We'll come back and clean everything up later. You can keep filming then. But, right now, we need to go over the next step with the group. Otherwise, we'll get caught. We barely got away last time when we killed one person."

Roseanne shut off the camera and exhaled her disappointment. "I get it." She stood and began toward Richard. Something was felt slipping over her head. Then there was a sudden tightening around her throat. She began to lift off the ground as the restriction became tighter. Fingers clawed at her neck as she choked. But they could not loosen her strangler. Desperate hands reached out to Richard for help.

He was absolutely terrified at what he was seeing. But it was not like he could do anything. There was nothing there. She was just floating in the air. A step back turned into him running away. A single scream let loose from his lips.

"Sounds like Richard is screaming?" Melody remarked in confusion. She would have fully expected Roseanne to be the one screaming if anything.

"Selling the scares," Zack explained with little supporting reason.

"I guess," Melody accepted anyway. "Whatever, let's go meet up with them."

They began to walk along. But did not get far when Melody felt her ankle be caught. "What the—?" was what she got out right before being cut off by a sharp zip. She was suddenly yanked back by her leg, slamming chin first on the ground before being dragged into darkness. Her screams echoed through the hall until abruptly becoming silent.

Zack was more confused than anything else. That made his attention to what just happened easily lost. He was drawn away by heavy breathing coming closer from the other direction. Turning discovered Richard running over in a panic.

"Something—" Richard's breath interrupted. "Something—" he mimed strangulation. "Something killed Roseanne."

"Bullshit," Zack blurted in disbelief.

"No. I'm not—" Richard was going to give a reason before noticing something odd, "Wait, where's Melody?"

Zack looked back in the direction she disappeared. Still skeptical, he said, "I can't believe you guys are trying to trick me."

"Oh god." Richard took Zack's statement as a sign that something happened to her. He turned to run away. There was a high-pressure release of air. In a blink, Richard was impaled against the wall by many pieces of rebar that pierced through his body.

Zack was no longer in a state of denial. In fact, terror overloaded his senses and he acted in flight. His feet propelled him into a full sprint down the hall in the direction of the exit. He reached the foyer in what seemed like seconds. He tried the doors to find them locked. He slammed his body against them, but they would not budge. There was no escape.

"What's the matter?" a voice called out.

Zack craned his neck around. There was nobody there. His eyes darted between the many dark corners that could conceal a presence.

Steven appeared from none of them. He had always been in the room, standing on a second-floor balcony, looking down into the foyer. It just took a moment to notice.

"You're alive!?" Zack blurted out in surprise and hope. "Where's Robert?"

"He's dead," Steven answered coldly.

Concern overtook. Zack wanted to question what happened. But the details did not matter. Just the facts.

184

"Something's happening. We need to get out of here before we're next."

"Why?" Asked Steven. "What happened to the others?"

"I don't know," Zack admitted. "Some . . . thing got them."

"What about Eve and Kyle?" Steven continued his interrogation.

"Well. . ?" Zack was sweating at the answer since, unlike what happened to the others, those two were murdered. "Like I said, something got them."

"Enough," Steven demanded the act be ended. "You killed them, didn't you?"

Zack had a sudden revelation. He wondered, "How did you know that?"

"Just like three years ago," Steven reminded.

"What the hell?" Zack was in shock. "How do you know that? Who are you?"

"No one of consequence," Steven commented. He pulled out a lighter and began to burn a scrap of paper. "Did you even smell the gas?" Then threw down the spark.

Jordan sat and watched the television intently with his heterochromia eyes of sea-foam-green and golden-hazel.

The newscaster reported, "Tonight a story that will rock the city of Darkess Noir. The once famous turned infamous Lorain Manor was set ablaze earlier this evening. The flames were extinguished before the building could be entirely destroyed. However, what the first responders discovered afterward was a gruesome scene of seven dead. Two were slain by an ax. Three were victims of wire traps. Another was killed by an air

185

cannon. And the last burned in the flames. The primary suspect for the fire and at least five of the murders is a former engineer by the name of Steven Townson. His whereabouts are currently unknown at this time.

"It is believed that Mr. Townson was enacting a form of revenge against the Haunt Hunters. Three years back, the original six members, Zack Porter, Melody Johnson, Richard Green, Robert Smith, Roseanne James, and Anthony Townson, went to Lorain Manor to conduct a paranormal investigation. Only five left. Anthony Townson, who we have determined to be the younger brother of Steven Townson, disappeared inexplicably. The police never closed the case.

"There was always speculation that the group was responsible in some way. However, without a body, there was no possibility to convict them of any crimes. Based on the current circumstances, it is fair to say they did in fact have something to do with the disappearance. Plenty of unedited video and audio evidence survived the fire detailing the murders of Eve Cane and Kyle Lo at the hands of Richard Green and Zack Porter. Fingerprints found on the murder weapons provided further evidence.

"Their motive was a simple one, the Haunt Hunters wanted attention. The group earned fame after the first disappearance, message boards filling with rumors while those interested in the paranormal looked to them as leading figures. But that fame was quick to fade. Over the years, they were long forgotten by their peers. These new killings are believed to be an attempt to regain their popularity. . ." The television continued to drone on and on with greater and greater detail that would make an amazing crime drama in the future.

"That's pretty horrific," Jordan said to Oswald. "Makes me feel uncomfortable. We just moved here, and a mass murder happens."

"I know what you mean," Oswald began to console. He pinched the scar on the bridge of his nose as he thought about what to follow up with, speaking stoically, "I know it's morbid of me to say, but there's one of these every day somewhere in the country. This one's just closer to home so it seems so much worse."

"I'm not going to let this get to me," Jordan assured. "I know you're right in your own depressing way. It's just unsettling. Though," having sympathy, "I actually get it. That guy, Steven was his name, wanted revenge on those that killed his brother just because they wanted their fifteen minutes. And they were going to do it again. If I had a brother, I might have done the same. So, I don't blame him as much as I blame them."

My Evil Twin

Heterochromia eyes of sea-foam-green and golden-hazel opened in the middle of the night, staring up into the nothing. Pupils slowly dilated as they adjusted to the darkness. Once everything was a vague shadow of itself, head turned to look at Oswald who was still sleeping soundly.

The man that was not Oswald got out of bed, taking some clothing before stepping out of the room. He dressed in the hall. Then a few minutes were used to look over social media to find a particular person.

He left the house as quietly as possible and did not risk taking the car. Luckily, he did not have that far to go. From the west suburb to the east suburb of Darkess was a thirty-minute walk through downtown.

Being by himself at night did not have him stand out. There were many people on the streets that made him not alone. Though the people of the city were rather reserved, a nightlife did exist. As the mom-and-pop stores closed their doors at six, half-a-dozen bars opened and stayed open well past midnight. As well, a couple of diners remained open twenty-four-seven to feed the drunk and hungry. Young crowds of mostly college students gathered downtown to meet those of their kind, along with desperate or alcoholic men and women, and the homeless that panhandled the late crowd.

Though downtown was the hub, it was still not suspicious for someone to be wandering around outside of the area. Plenty of people lived close enough to drunkenly stumble their way home. None would really question the sweater-hooded figure walking through the dim neighborhood.

The hooded figure knocked on the door of a degrading home. The striking of his knuckles against the metal was commanding but not that loud. It demanded the occupants of the house to respond but did not call the attention of the neighbors. When there was no answer after a minute, there would be another knock, and again until someone responded.

The door flung open after three knocks. On the other side of the aperture stood an old, white man, a bit on the heavy-set side, who had a permanent frown. He barked, "What the hell do you want! It's fucking twelve—!"

Mismatched eyes stared imposing from the shadows beneath the hood. The old man was left paralyzed with fear for a split second. That fear held him in place as a small twenty-two pistol was pointed directly at his head. A single pull of the trigger popped. The sound was loud but not one of concern, more a curiosity as long as there were not more of them. Anybody who heard would most likely forget right away. And there would be no need to shoot a second time as the single bullet obliterated the old man's brain.

The figure turned and walked away.

Jordan leaned over the cadaver that had most recently entered his autopsy room. He did not express much outward emotion but did feel a sense of contentment. A thousand faces had been seen and forgotten but this permanent frown, even in death, was one he was familiar with. There was no forgetting so soon after how angry it made him. Some days back, this old man had yelled homophobic slurs.

Jamie Gram, a gritty gumshoe, leaned in next to Jordan, intruding personal space, to make a personal assessment of the body as well.

189

"Do you need to be here, detective?" Jordan asked, partly annoyed and partly preferring to work alone when work needed to be done. He was well-aware of his own extraverted shortcomings, getting lost in conversation when there was someone to talk to. Less tended to get done when that happened. He then tacked on, "Also, would you not get so close."

Detective Gram gazed at Jordan for a moment in plain contemplation before lifting away from the body and stepping back from the table. Then he remarked to the initial question, "You're the primary coroner now which means we'll be working together a lot. Best I get to know you sooner rather than later."

"Are you saying that violent crime isn't uncommon here?" Jordan questioned the implication.

"Murders don't happen that often . . ." Detective Gram stated before debating with himself on how much to say. Knowing that getting to know somebody was a two-way street, he chose to be honest, "No point pretending otherwise. The violent crime rates here aren't much different from most other cities. However, when these crimes are committed, they more often than not happen all around the same time."

Jordan sunk into his thoughts for a moment as he recognized that that situation was happening. He looked toward the cooling shelves aware that eight of them were occupied. All those people, as well as the one currently laid out on the table, died yesterday.

Seven bodies were victims of the Lorain Manor incident. They had yet to be examined or processed mainly due to the fact that the victims and suspects were already determined. Further evidence might bring to light new information but there was little need for that right away. The unsolved crime was of higher priority.

The eighth outlier that came in was a drowned man. The incident was ruled an accident by EMTs and corroborated by a survivor, the man's mistress. However, there was bruising found on his legs that closely resembled hands as if he was grabbed and pulled under the water. An in-depth examination would be needed. However, no additional deaths were expected to occur around this individual. Again, the unsolved crime was of higher priority.

Thinking about those cases had Jordan recalled the three other incidents and four other bodies that came to him within the week.

Days back, two women had killed themselves on the very same evening. Their deaths were fully determined to be suicides, yet the circumstances were questionable. Sophia Nightingale did have a history of depression making her death plausible. But Claire Pontain seemed to have no motivations as she was well-off, with a succeeding career, plenty of loved ones, and no history of mental illness. What they did share was an affiliation with Jack Solomon having both been with him on the same day they died. However, the authorities concluded that he had no involvement.

The realization struck that Jack Solomon was the same man that Jordan was painted by the day before. Jordan worried. He was sure the connection to those deaths was coincidental. He was the one that did the autopsies and made the final decision after all. Surely, he would not die inexplicably. But a little paranoia gave him a chill.

Thought returned to the previous concern.

There was also the body of a different old man that came in at an even earlier time. He had been struck on the head, strangled, and raped. His cause of death was strangulation and was ruled a murder. The suspect should have been easy enough to find with the abundant amount of DNA evidence. However, oddly, the semen found was his own. His case remains open, but the examination has already been conducted.

Then there was no forgetting the very first body that Jordan worked on. Travis Polt's death has since been ruled an accident. However, the fact of the matter was his autopsy never concluded because of the parasite issue. Jordan continued to be skeptical since, from his initial findings, there was evidence that appeared to contradict the accidental nature of the death. But, with Dr. Trime already making the final determination, there was nothing further to be done.

"Is that what's going on right now?" Jordan asked. "I've been here for a week and twelve bodies— Well," he clarified, "twelve deaths under suspicious circumstances have been brought to me. I've seen more than twelve bodies."

"Things should calm down soon," Detective Gram assured.

"That's good to hear," Jordan was thankful. "I didn't expect so much overflow for my first week and I was getting worried."

"Don't be grateful just yet," Detective Gram warned. "There will be more if we don't find the culprit of this crime, soon. But, aside from that, yes, Darkess should quiet down for a bit."

"I'll find whatever evidence there is," Jordan guaranteed. "So, who do we have here?"

"This is the body of Tucker Sheldon," Detective Gram introduced. "A single gunshot wound to the head with what appears to be a twenty-two. Died instantly. His body was found early this morning. However, witnesses say they heard a 'pop' late in the night but dismissed the sound. I'd say he was killed around one o'clock."

"Geeze," Jordan uttered, "I just asked for a name. Looks like you did all the work for me."

"He's a rather hated man," the detective added on, ignoring the jesting remark.

"I'm not surprised." Jordan admitted, "I actually recognize this guy. He harassed me and my boyfriend while we were downtown."

"A story I've heard before," Detective Gram detailed. "He's as much a homophobe as he is a racist and a sexist."

"Men like this are always that trifecta, aren't they?" Jordan made commentary on the state of hate.

"Must have offended you."

"Of course," Jordan spoke honestly. "I wanted to hit him in his stupid face. But I had Oswald with me, and he calmed me down."

"Looks like I can add you to the list of suspects," Detective Gram deadpannedly informed.

"Funny," Jordan winced a small smile at the remark. But then looking at Detective Gram realized, by his expression, "Wait, you're being serious."

"It's only procedure," Detective Gram ensured.

"Then should I even be conducting the autopsy?" Jordan raised the question.

"Keep working," the detective ushered Jordan to continue what he was doing. "I'm certain you're not the guilty party. I'm just keeping the possibility open to cover all my bases."

Jordan gave a perplexed look, shook his head, and returned to his examination. "I'll let you know what I find once I'm done," the comment intended to excuse the detective from the room, who did do just that.

"How was work?" Oswald asked at the dinner table since this was the first chance he had gotten to do so.

193

Jordan ended up working for nearly fourteen hours straight and did not get back home until nine o'clock. He was tired and maybe even a little cracked after having to cut up more than the normal number of bodies in a day, which was often not even one person. Today he dissected four. Then there were the examinations of everybody that also included the needed paperwork. The moment he got home, he was left alone to relax out of work mode. He took a long shower and dressed down into sweats. Even at the table, he seemed disinterested in any interaction. He answered anyway, "Way too much for one day."

"I'm sorry," Oswald apologized for the circumstance. "We'll keep the night calm. Hopefully, tomorrow won't be as trying."

"Thanks," Jordan returned the courtesy. "Tomorrow should be fine. I stayed late to make sure I wouldn't have as much to do when I went back in. But enough about me and enough about work. How was your day?"

"Are you sure you're okay?" Oswald pressed the subject of work anyway. He knew Jordan well enough that there was much more that wanted to be voiced. "I want to make sure everything's alright."

"Well," Jordan contemplated before continuing, "It's all alright. It's just . . . not like I haven't had to cut up so many bodies before. I just hate how I suddenly have so many more responsibilities. I literally started working at this hospital a week ago and, turns out, I didn't even realize this, I'm the lead coroner now. Which makes sense I guess because the salary is good. But they never told me that would be the case. When I applied, they said I would be taking an upper staff position, not that I'd be taking over the entire department."

"That is asking a lot without telling you," Oswald sympathized. "You could," he was sheepish to say, "ask to be a lower position. Or even quit."

"I could," Jordan played with the idea. "You're making enough to take care of the both of us for the time being. But I don't actually want to quit. I just feel like I'm being taken advantage of. There's literally only one other coroner employed just so that I can have days off. But, because we never work together, I don't know how much they actually do, and if they're even good at their job. Then there's Dr. Trime who sometimes works in the morgue. I know she's good at her job or she wouldn't have the position she does. But I kind of think she's covering up details about deaths. She constantly throws my observations into question. So, I feel like I have to do everything just to be thorough.

"But the most annoying thing to happen today was the lead detective actually said I'm a possible suspect in one of the cases."

"Why?" Oswald asked in confusion.

"Because one of the victims that came in today was that homophobe that harassed us," Jordan reminded. "I mentioned that and suddenly the detective is thinking I might have something to do with it. He probably has you as a suspect too. I don't like being accused of something I obviously didn't do. Who would really murder over something so petty?

"Alright," Jordan expressed positively. "Thanks for letting me vent. I'm feeling so much better. Now, how was your day?"

"Great for the most part," Oswald switched the subject. "It's been a week since classes started and, like I said in the beginning, every student seems committed to their studies. So much better than that year I was doing my work studies."

"I remember you complaining every day how nobody had any real interest in the class," Jordan recalled. "They were just there for the credits."

Oswald sighed and spoke of his past frustrations, "Their work was always half-assed. And when marked for their mistakes they become confrontational as if they knew more than me, the teacher. TA," he corrected. "I'm not even talking about the subject matter. I'd find a grammatical error on an assignment and, instead of that student learning the proper spelling or phrasing, they would say I was wrong, and then continue to make the mistake. And these were college students." He shook his head in disappointment.

"You went off like this before." Jordan smiled at the nostalgic moment.

Oswald smiled back. "It's a lot better here."

Jordan continued to smile. "That makes me happy." Then he wondered, "You said 'great for the most part.' What wasn't great?"

"Well," Oswald recounted, "The students are good but there was this one entitled mother that came to see me. The whole situation was awkward and upsetting by the end. She wanted her kid in my class, but the class is full and there are a few other students on the waitlist before hers." Oswald began to cringe as he shook his head in disapproval at the thought. "She offered sexual favors to get her kid in. I turned her down for a million reasons. Then she tried to threaten me to get her kid in the class by coming up with this lie that I was the one asking for the favors to allow her kid in my class. I told her I was gay, so that lie would definitely not work. That made her mad because she couldn't manipulate me. And, before storming off, she called me a faggot. The whole thing . . ." he did not even know how to end the retelling.

Jordan was shocked. "That pisses me off."

"Don't," Oswald really hoped. "It's dealt with. No need to push the matter anymore. I honestly want to move on already because it's just embarrassing in a gross way."

Jordan would not bring the subject up again. But for the rest of the evening, he was in constant angry contemplation in the back of his mind.

That night there was another murder.

A mature woman was laid on the examination table, deceased, but her body was still warm.

"Amber Roberson," Detective Gram identified. "She was killed approximately two hours ago, around five this morning while on her way to work. A single shot to the head like Tucker Sheldon by a twenty-two. This is most likely the same gun. Forensics is still running ballistic comparisons, but there has been a discovery when searching the ballistic database. Turns out the weapon used in the first crime is linked to four unsolved murders that happened in Everette. You moved from Everette, didn't you?"

"I did," Jordan answered plainly, more focused on the examination, "but I don't believe I worked on those cases. Providence Hospital had a larger staff of medical examiners to divvy up our intake. I'd probably remember since a coroner assigned to a crime does all the autopsy for the case to keep things consistent."

Detective Gram intently inspected every word said until satisfied that he heard the truth. He continued his assessment, "Witnesses heard a 'pop' but didn't dismiss the sound like before. More than likely because the news ran the story of Tucker Sheldon and people are remaining aware of gunshots. However, they didn't immediately call nine-one-one either. Bystanders took it upon themselves to look for the body first, which they found. And because we," referring to the authorities, "got the call late, searching for a suspect became needless."

"So, no witnesses?" Jordan assumed.

"That's not entirely true," Detective Gram revealed. Jordan looked up out of curiosity, not concern. The detail was given, "At approximately one o'clock, there was a knock at Amber Roberson's door. Her husband answered but found nobody. The culprit most likely expected the same tactic wouldn't have worked twice but still made the attempt more cautiously, hiding out of sight. At least, out of sight of the house's occupants. A neighbor witnessed a hooded figure by the bushes. We're getting a facial composition made right now at the station. Even if the details are lacking, we should be able to use street cameras to find and follow suspects that closely resemble the sketch."

"Kind of amazing," Jordan expressed both skepticism and fascination. "And a little unsettling. It's like we're always being watched. Feels so intrusive but I get it."

Detective Gram had not expected the reaction or the comments that followed. He blatantly questioned, "Do you know the victim?"

"I do not," Jordan answered plainly.

"What were you doing last night?" The detective continued grilling.

"Sleeping," Jordan answered right away before irritably remarking, "You're seriously going to interrogate me? I know you said I was a suspect. But you also said that was just procedure and you didn't think I was actually responsible. Do we need to do the questioning?"

"Where were you this morning?"

"Sleeping before heading to work," Jordan humored. "Anything else?"

"There's something you're hiding," Detective Gram pressured.

Jordan gave a deflated look as he was getting upset by the accusations. "I really don't know what you're talking about."

Detective Gram knew for a fact that Jordan was the culprit of these crimes. The evidence had already been found, motive, means, and opportunity. The detective had his hunch right from the beginning, and the legitimacy of his belief was proven by the sharp pain on the tip of his middle finger. That prophetic sense had never once been wrong.

A stakeout witnessed Jordan leave his house twice, once around midnight, lining up with the unknown visitor the Robersons had, and the other at four in the morning, lining up with the actual crime. Though he had not been witnessed during either incident, somehow slipping away from the police detail, his whereabouts were determined later no more than blocks away. That gave opportunity.

For means, the ballistics search that linked the weapon to the unsolved crimes in Everett found that the gun once belonged to a petty criminal named Daniel Douglas. He had died while committing a convenience store robbery. Shot three times in the chest by the cashier, he was rushed to the hospital where he succumbed to his injuries. The body was sent to the morgue and Jordan was the one that conducted the autopsy. The gun that Daniel used during his crime was never recovered from the scene, nor confiscated by the EMTs or doctors, and was never reported by the coroner, Jordan. The weapon simply disappeared.

For motive, Jordan's spouse, Oswald Rook, and the victim, Amber Roberson, were heard having a heated argument the day before. The details remained undetermined at this time but would be looked further into once an official arrest had been made.

Detective Gram was about to make his move when—

"Twins," the announcement came from Dr. Trime who stood in the doorway of the autopsy room. Both Jordan and the detective reflexively looked her way. Her arrival was unexpected, and she had appeared unnoticed until now.

Detective Gram wondered, "What about twins?"

"Dr. Setly has heterochromia eyes," she explained. "That often occurs when fraternal twins are developing in the womb and one of them absorbs the other."

"I know," Jordan replied, trying his best to not sound snarky as he followed up with, "I did go to medical school." Then he became a bit gloomy, saying, "I always felt bad about it."

"Doctor?" Detective Gram sought an explanation.

Dr. Trime spoke directly to the detective, "You brought me the information about these recent crimes and I decided to do a bit of research on my own. I wish to discuss my findings. If you would excuse us, Dr. Setly."

"By all means," Jordan preferred them to go so he could better focus.

Detective Jamie Gram took a drag from his cigarette and blew the smoke into the wind. It was always cold and windy on the hospital roof. But this was where to be right now. This place had the most privacy. And this was the only place Emilia Trime allowed him to smoke when on hospital grounds, even though he was technically breaking the law.

"What's this about, Emilia?" Jamie asked, using her first name to express familiarity.

"You'll need to cover up Dr. Setly's crimes," Emilia ordered.

"I can't just do that for anybody," he stated.

"Dr. Setly is far from just anybody," she guaranteed. "He himself is not even aware that he committed those crimes. Factually speaking, he didn't commit them."

"Explain," the detective demanded.

"Two souls exist within that young man—" she started.

"He's bipolar?" Jamie attempted to simplify the definition.

"That's a mental health issue that can be regulated with medication," she clarified. "A second soul isn't something that can be controlled. It has a will of its own."

"Even so," he cared not, "that doesn't dismiss the crime."

"It wouldn't dismiss the crimes of a stranger," she understood. "But Jordan Setly is family to Darkess Noir just like Jesse Dox Junior, Caeseal Wood, Elain Cane, and our Coven of Witches to name a few. Each of them has committed crimes that you needed to overlook."

"What makes Jordan Setly family?" Jamie still needed something definitive.

"By definition, a second soul is a guardian spirit, one similar to yourself," she compared. "This city is a haven for the unearthly and arcane. Gods live in our forests and waters. Some protect knowledge while others bring death. Neither is condemned for committing to their nature. Nor should Dr. Setly."

"The Gods do as they please but not the unbound spirits," he countered. "Junior is a child of Gluttony.

201

Caeseal and Elain are acolytes of Nemesis. But Jordan has no affiliations that protect him."

"What of Oswald Rook?" Emilia posed. "His family founded this city. Mortal or not, the Gods have always considered the Rook family their ally and one of their equals. If Jordan and Jordan's second soul are bound to a person, they are bound to him."

Detective Jamie Gram finally heard something compelling even though he did not like it. He lit another cigarette, "I'll see what I can do."

Final Offering

A night, black and lonely. Not a person or car on the street, not a star, not even the moon in the sky. The storm clouds blocked out the light and the rain they brought chased nearly everyone and everything away. There was only Oswald sheltered beneath an umbrella.

He stood on the bridge that both connected the worlds and divided them. The westside of Darkess was solely joined to downtown and the eastside by the concrete road. The Puget Sound was forever separated from Municipal Lake by that bridge and the mechanisms of a dam. An incomplete crossroad between man and nature. The perfect conduit that allowed otherworldly entities to come and go without letting people unintentionally pass through and be forever lost in another reality.

Oswald stared intently at the lake. He did not know where he was or how he got here, nor did he find himself concerned in the least. Watching the heavy rain scatter the surface and sounding like static was tranquil.

His own reflection, a reflection that should not have been possible, stared up at him and asked, "Would you like to be a God?"

He had no response.

His reflection, standing on the surface of the water, asked again, "Would you like to be a God?"

He had no response.

His reflection stood next to him on the bridge, speaking, "I asked you if you would like to be a God. Aren't you ever going to answer?"

Oswald looked up to the sky from just under the brim of the tilted umbrella as he pondered. But the thoughts eluded him. There had been many times he wanted to be God for just a moment. There had been many deeds considered in great detail, what he would do for the world, what he would say to the people. There had been a perfect reality designed in his mind. Yet, none of this came to him now. He feared that if he was to speak, even as a hypothetical God, his words would then exist, and, had someone heard them, he would bear the responsibility of what followed.

"You need to speak," his reflection urged. "Even if you hide in silence for your whole life, I'll still be here waiting for your answer in your next one."

Oswald began with related small talk, "I'm pretty sure everybody has thought about being God at least once."

"Most certainly," his reflection agreed. "But not all are deserving."

"What makes me deserving?" He questioned.

"Nobody said you were," his reflection replied. "This is an offer at the chance, not a guarantee."

"That means I would have to prove myself worthy if I did decide I wanted to be God?" He predicted what entailed and held reservations. "That alone gives me a reason to say no. I prefer to avoid making an attempt at something that is far from possible."

"You would give up on greatness because it demands effort to achieve?" His reflection raised the disappointing fact. "You would only accept being God if given and not earned?"

"I'm just lazy, I guess."

"Well," his reflection deliberated, "I did not say the attempt would be difficult. In fact, perhaps it is as simple as answering a few questions?"

"Then my answer would be no to being God," Oswald said definitively.

"Why?"

"Because becoming God should not be easy," Oswald felt.

"But you already said you were uninterested in something too difficult," the reflection reminded. "You're contradicting yourself."

"That's the exact reason I don't feel I deserve to be God," he told only half the truth before admitting, "I'm being facetious. Honestly, I've always worked hard toward the goals that I want. But I don't know if I want to truly be God."

"But why?" His reflection wondered.

"Too much responsibility." Oswald paused again for this was what he had been having difficulty talking about. He knew he needed to give his reasons regardless if they came out jumbled or lacking clarity. "If I were God, I would want to speak directly to the people and let them know full well what they should be doing . . . but it's not easy to explain what they should be doing. Actions and ideas are not simply good or bad. There are things that go without question, but more often the morality of what is done is less determined by itself and more by the motivation leading up to the action. So, how would I convey what I mean? Should I talk to them the way I'm talking to you right now?" He smirked at the ridiculous idea. "Being a God so proactively involved in the lives of others absolutely takes the mystique away."

"There has not been a God like that before," his reflection acknowledged. "But I don't see why you would not succeed as such."

"A God like that would require a certain demeanor upheld at all times," he expanded on the notion of such a God. "You have to speak eloquently to show greatness that commands worship yet speak simply for everybody to understand completely. You cannot second guess your decisions or go back on them once they've already been made. You must remember everything you have already done on the day they were done. You'd need to be perfect. I couldn't maintain that forever. And it would have to be forever.

"Not to forget that there will still be those that hear what I say and, though I may be the voice of God, they would not agree with my views and label me the devil instead. Let's face it, pride, the pride of a religious zealot expects God to fulfill their desires instead of adhering to the values of their God."

"Then why do it that way?" His reflection disputed. "Be a God like the rest."

"The at-a-distance way has too much nuance," he dismissed. "You look at religion right now and see how it struggles. It's exactly as I just said. People make their own interpretations that best suit them. Then they ignore any instructions that inconvenience them. Or they just make stuff up because, let's be honest, nobody knows anything about their own religion. Someone just told it to someone who told it to them. All this to justify persecuting others they are threatened by, or just generally don't like. This has been the result of not leading the people and, instead, expecting others to follow a guidebook." Then said to himself, under his breath but full of sympathy, "I wonder how that God must feel seeing what has become of their attempt?"

The reflection absorbed the negativity of those words. Slowly, its tone changed, looking less like his mirror image and more like his shadow. "What if I had another offer? You could end the existence of all the Gods."

Oswald took a casual breath while he thought even though he knew the answer. "No. God . . . the Gods are not to blame for what's wrong with the world, no matter how much people wish to blame them. I've heard many people say countless times how if Gods didn't exist then there would be no more violence. Of course, there would. There has been violence since the beginning of mankind. That's because people are really to blame."

"Would you want to end the existence of all people?" His shadow presented another option. "Restart the world and make one where there is no evil."

"I should say," Oswald continued from where he left off instead of answering, "most people aren't to blame either. They're often desperate for answers that will never be found and are fooled into thinking one man, one book, or one organization really has those answers. It's that small few who do the deceiving that ruins the world for the rest. Instead of the ideals of a God, it's their ideals that are reinterpreted by those who listened to them. So, to answer your question, No. Ending the existence of everyone to spite a terrible few would not be the right thing to do."

"Then destroy those few," the shadow offered the solution.

"Ruling through fear just like the Old Testament?" Oswald considered. "Apparently, it does work. Not many actually see that God as evil. But would I be so lucky? No. No, because it isn't about luck. Selfish people only like a God that punishes the people they don't agree with. But if I were to punish the selfish, I would just become the Devil like I already said. And no matter how many of them I got rid of, someone else would take up that role right after with identical ideals, if not more warped, and continue to blame me."

"You see nothing good," his shadow recognized. "Not even in those who are fooled."

"Yes," he acknowledged, "but no. I'm certainly Nihilistic. But there is good. For some people, finding direction in the world is difficult and they need guidance whether it be right or wrong. Some will learn to help others. Some will choose to harm. But those who harm either get what they deserve or learn where they went wrong and find some kind of redemption. No matter how bad things are, we move slowly toward a better world. So, I could be a God, try to change the world, and risk making things worse. Or I can let the world change gradually on its own. The latter seems the best option."

"But not everybody gets what they deserve," his shadow argued.

"That can't be helped," he showed more of his nihilistic optimism. "Though we might not like it, bad people deserve a little good too. I'm not saying we give it to them. But, after the fight is done and every chance to bring justice has been exhausted, if they're still standing, fight even more until you can no longer, and then sure, definitely be upset if you lose, but don't think the world is to blame."

The darkness of the shadow stopped deepening and slowly began to regress in tone. "You do not want to be a God. Nor do you want to see them gone. Nor do you want to rid the world of humans. What do you want?"

"I just want to stay where I am," Oswald accepted. "Maybe if I was a God, I could change the world. But that requires people to listen to me. Some would. Some won't. Others would reinterpret my message. And other others would see me negatively. There are still so many limitations, more limitations if anything by having endless power. In the end, there really is nothing different between being a God and being Oswald. Only the scale of my existence would change. However, by being me I get to retain what is important to me. My job. My family. My Jordan. But being God, those get pushed aside and must share importance with everything else that's within my power of influence. I would have to sacrifice my personal happiness and what makes me myself. I'd rather change the world in a small way and take care of my few responsibilities."

"The same answer as before," his reflection pronounced with satisfaction. "I'm glad to see you have yet to change."

Oswald felt a wave of familiarity. "Have we met before?"

"Of course," his reflection swore. "Though last we met was long ago in the body of a woman."

"Elise Rook?" He assumed.

"She was the very first of you that I spoke to," his reflection revealed. "But she was not the last. She had a daughter. And her daughter had a daughter. That version of you was the last time we spoke."

"Who are you, again?" He could not remember as he began softly pounding on the side of his head to remember.

"I am you. I am your entire bloodline. I am the idea of Godhood personified by the powers of the other Gods who respect you, your family."

The reflection raised a finger and pressed the tip on the small scar that ran across the bridge of Oswald's nose. Memories of every generation before, every feeling felt, that of pain and pleasure, beauty seen and disgust understood, rushed through him rapidly until the experience became nothing more than a drop of water. The corporal collection of his family's experiences landed with a pluck into the vast body of water that was everyone and everything else in the world. But that too became as small as a drop. Everything shrunk and shrunk as everything grew and grew to soon be what was the solar system, to the galaxy, the universe itself. And even the universe became nothing in the ever-expanding blackness of nothingness until there was a spark of light. Moving toward this beacon, Oswald was born from the womb of his mother once more and his life flashed before his eyes. The finger retracted and with it the power, "But I cannot truly exist yet until you're ready. Therefore, I shall come again with this offer in your next life, for your next kin. Until then."

"Will I ever be ready?" Oswald questioned before this dream came to an end.

"What do you call the God of Humility?" The reflection asked a little riddle in place of an answer.

"A man."

"In our eyes, you're already ready," the reflection assured. "You just need to make the decision when you yourself want this."

"Then would there ever be a day that I am not?"

"With a question like that, I'd say no."

Fingers snapped.

Oswald woke in his bed beside Jordan and just stared blankly up at the ceiling for an hour.

When Jordan woke and saw Oswald already awake, he commented, "Good morning."

Oswald was freed from his paralysis, shaking his head while scrunching his face and wiping one eye. Then he replied with, "I had the strangest dream. Maybe it was a nightmare. Definitely something existential." He yawned.

"What was it about?" Jordan wanted to understand so that he might provide some comfort.

"I can't really remember," Oswald admitted as he thought back to the dream but only found a black space in his mind sounding of static.

"I hate that," Jordan expressed. "Why do we forget our dreams right away?"

"Well," Oswald shrugged. "It mustn't have been as important as waking up next to you, or I would have remembered. Or maybe I'm still dreaming because I have an angel next to me."

Jordan snuggled close and the two rested for just a second more in each other's arms. Life was good.